T0168897

THE LAST OF THE OFOS

Volume 39

Sun Tracks
An American Indian Literary Series

Series Editor
Ofelia Zepeda

Editorial Committee
Vine Deloria, Jr.
Larry Evers
Joy Harjo
N. Scott Momaday
Emory Sekaquaptewa
Leslie Marmon Silko

THE LAST

of the

OFOS

Geary Hobson

THE UNIVERSITY OF ARIZONA PRESS   TUCSON

First printing

The University of Arizona Press

© 2000 Geary Hobson

All rights reserved

♾ This book is printed on acid-free, archival-quality paper.

Manufactured in the United States of America

05   04   03   02   01   00   6   5   4   3   2   1

Library of Congress Cataloging-in-Publication Data

Hobson, Geary.

The last of the Ofos / Geary Hobson.

p. cm. — (Sun tracks ; v. 39)

ISBN 0-8165-1958-7 (alk. paper)

ISBN 0-8165-1959-5 (pbk.: alk. paper)

1. Indians of North America—Louisiana Fiction

I. Title. II. Series.

PS501.S85 vol.39 PS3558.O336937

810.8 s—dc21   99-6472

[813'.54]   CIP

British Library Cataloguing-in-Publication Data

A catalogue record for this book is available from the British Library.

We have a promise from the Sun. As long as there

is the Sun, there will be Indian people here.

—Chief Joseph Alcide Pierite

("Chief Joe"; c. 1874–1976),

Chief of the Tunica Indians, 1955–1975

Contents

The Last of the Ofos

The Mosopelea, or Ofo, Tribe was always a small tribe, never more than a few hundred people, from the time of first white contact with them in the late 1600s until their demise in the early twentieth century. They were a peaceful people who spoke a strange Siouan language and lived out their existence through centuries of turbulence and change in the lush Mississippi delta land dominated by their haughty and more numerous Muskhogean and Tunican neighbors. When the Ofos passed on as a people, they left little behind them except those works of human history and existence which Indian folks claim can still be heard at certain moments of late afternoons and early evenings, as wind drifts through cypress and sweet gum in certain special ways, and in barely perceptible ripples made suddenly and unaccountably in the backwater bayous of the Mississippi alluvial country in early mornings when Sun Father blesses all that is before Him. These ripples and breezes, folks say, are spirits of long-ago Ofos speaking. Mrs. Rosa Pierrette of Marksville, Louisiana, was the last speaker of her tribe's language, and the last actual Ofo. For the purposes of my story, however, I call on Thomas Darko, an Ofo of my imagination, to embody the enduring history of his and Mrs. Pierrette's people. Rosa Pierrette died in 1915, and it is to her memory, and to all her descendants among the Tunica-Biloxi people still residing in Louisiana, that this story is humbly and respectfully dedicated.

I

Out of the Earth at Ofo Town

I guess if I-mo tell you my life story, I got to start way back at the
very beginning, about when and where I was born and all that
kind of thing. But since all that come down to me second-hand
from my folks now long passed away, I guess I ought to start at a
later time. Besides, since all them first-this and first-that kind of
things probly ain't all that interesting to hear, even if I could recall
them clearly—about my first breath of Mother Earth's good air,
my first drink of milk, my first words, first memories, and what-
all—they'll probly all come out anyhow as the story gits told. And
if it don't, then I spect it don't matter none.

Jist to think about it for a minute: like, when was the first
time I ever heared the sound that a sorrowbird make late in the
evening after the sun has went down? Shoot, I don't know. And
they's no way I could even start to recall. Or, when was the first
time I ever smelled cotton in the autumn time, like how it, the
seed-oily smell and the dust, carries in the air all through the
countryside along with the whine of the gins jist before they shut
down for the day? I don't know when that could of been neither.

Or, you could jist as easy ask when was the first time I ever watch a water moccasin glide graceful-like across the top of a bayou's black water? They's no way I can answer any of these questions—except to say that all these things was always there, for me to know them and for me to learn them. Always and for all time they was a part of my life and the world I was a part of. *Was* a part of. Now that's righter than I ever wanted it to be. Cause things has sho changed a whole goddamned lot since I was little.

Oh, a word of warning: I talk dirty. Don't let them tell you Indians don't cuss. We do—whenever we need to.

Anyways, it would be easier to separate the bark from the tree trunk—or stink from shit, as my papa used to say—than it would be for you to set me aside from my land and all my earliest memories of it. Cause till the time I reached my twenties, jist before the Big Depression come on, I hadn't never been away from my home more than jist a few days at a time. But that's all a long ways back—way back, in the past. Since then, I been a lot of places, been in some foreign countries, even, and in nearly every one of the states of the United States. I had a lot of adventures, too. I run whiskey; I worked the wheat fields some all through the Great Plains; I butchered livestock in Fort Worth. I roustabouted and drilled in near-bout ever oil field in Louisiana. Shoot, for a while I even farted around as a rodeo clown out in New Mexico and Texas. Was a time, too, I dug taters in Colorado and Nebraska, and part of another year I like to froze my tail off working construction on the Alcan Highway up in the Yukon country. And they was that time, too, when I waded through a mile of ocean surf at Tarawa, facing Jap machine-gun bullets, sho my time was up and a death song on my lips. I walked some real-mean streets in big cities like Chicago and Washington, D.C., and K.C. and Memphis and New

Orleans—always carrying with me a loaded .38 pistol or sometime a straight-razor. Most times I carried both. I even went out to Hollywood one time to be in a picture-show about feather-bonnet Indians, and I even pretended to be one, jist so I could git the job, and I got it, too, and some other ones besides. Another time, jist cause I got a Louisiana accent, they had me play a Cajun in a show about jazz music. You got to of lived through the 1930s and 1940s to know what I mean. And you got to be Indian, jist like I am, to know how much that galls—that having to act like you was something else other than what you be.

But all this is still not the real beginning. All this that I said so far that's done taken up near-bout a half a roll on this new tape recorder, all this talking about first hearing certain things, or smelling certain things, and talking about where I been and all, don't seem like a proper start, so I guess I-mo start all over.

To begin again: I am Thomas Darko, and I come from Sherrillton, Louisiana. I was born in the year 1905. Actually, I was born two mile outside the town of Sherrillton, which is pretty much a Cajun town in the plumb-near middle of the state, but in the eastern part and a few mile from where the Red River joins the Mississippi. I was born Ashohá, which in my Indian language means plover, and I was born for the Bird Clan of the Mosopelea tribe—a tribe which white people way back yonder insisted on calling Ofo. A plover, as I know you know, is a little brown bird— what some people call dull-looking, but that's jist cover, cause they be real smart and know how to survive aginst the bigger things around them.

I am the sixth kid of Baptiste and Josephine Darko. My father, of the Bird Clan, was the son of a Cajun man, Emile Darko— only he spelt it different from what I do now, but I don't know how it was—and Marie Registe, a full-blood woman of the Bird Clan of the Mosopelea Tribe. My great-grandpapa, Louis Registe, was headman of our tribe for many years. I never knowed him since he died sometime back in the 1880s. Since our clanship come from our father's side, my papa was adopted by the Bird people of his mother—what they would do most times when a baby's papa was a white man—but he growed up all Indian. My mother was Josephine Arceneaux of the Snake Clan, and they was some French blood in her, too, way back there, but not enough I reckon to worry none over. Her papa, my grandpapa, Louis Arceneaux, was headman of all the Mosopelea all the time I was a boy growing up. Fact is, he was also one of the headmen with the Tunicas, too, who we was counted amongst, since he had some Tunica blood, too. From my great-grandmama Arceneaux, I think it come from.

My brothers and sisters was: Leland, ten year older than me, Andrew, six year older than me, Baptiste Junior, three year older than me, Martha and Marie, twin sisters two year older than me, and Camille, the littlest, two year younger than me. They all had Mosopelea names, too, but I won't tell them out loud since they and they names have all passed on now and in our old way that wouldn't be proper.

Off and on, too, we would have Tunica or Biloxi cousins stay with us, so that at almost any time of the year we be a whole houseload of folks.

Now Ofo is our own word, but somehow some early anthropologist come up with the notion it was a Choctaw and Chickasaw word, and that in the old days they called us that name in they language for dogs because, at least according to what that feller wrote, they—them Chocks I'm talking about—had so little

6

regard for us as people that they thought of us as that—dogs. I guess. But I really won't swear to it. I met a lot of Choctaws and Chickasaws in my time, and they was pure-D good people, for the most part. But people we shore was—*are*. Although now, of course, as you all know, I am a nation of one. I am, so say that guidebook in the Museum of the American Indian in New York City, "The Last of the Ofos."

But it wudn't always this way. When I was growing up back then, we was all a great-big family. They was Mama and Papa and my six brothers and sisters, like I mentioned, my grandpapa, and even a couple of Tunica and Biloxi cousins who stayed with us. With about a dozen to fifteen families of Tunicas and Biloxis, we all lived in about that many houses on Indian land about the size of a postage stamp that the state of Louisiana begrudged us as our own. Because nearly all of us in our family spoke that Ofo language before we learned any English or coon-ass French, and even Tunica, we had our house and a handful of out-buildings off at the end of the settlement, and we was considered part of the Tunica and Biloxi tribe, even if we seen ourselves as a separate tribe—we was a tribe in a tribe, you might say. They was a handful of Biloxi people, too, but they ain't got they own language no more.

Our little place was called Ofo Town. Our total holdings wudn't no more that two acres, although the Tunicas, a lot of them our relatives, had a whole lot more. Time was, all us— Tunicas, Choctaws, Chitimachas, Biloxis, Houmas, Atakapas, Ofos—we used to own the whole damn state of Louisiana and now our combined lands all be about the size of a gnat's ass. It's sure a hell of a note when you consider that Indians once owned this whole damn continent and now we lucky can we git six-foot-

7

down of it when we pass on to the Great Beyond. Yes-sir, it be a hell of a note.

Papa was a fisherman for jist about half of the year and a trapper for the other half of the year. So was my uncles and grandpapa. Fact, so was nearly all the other folks in that part of the country. We taken our living out of the swamps and bayous—all kinds of catfish and other fish, and coon, mink, possum, squirrel, bear, fox, mushrat, alligator, wild hog, deer—for years and years. Papa also farmed a little cotton and corn and pumpkins. Mama used to sell the pumpkins, along with some piddly little split-cane baskets she make, under a little roadside shed that my oldest brother, Leland, built for her, and Papa sold the cotton down to the gin in Sherrillton, but he always keep the corn for whiskey. Mama used to complain about all that corn getting turned into whiskey.

She say, "I-swear, Baptiste. All that good corn made into whiskey. Let me have some of it for the hogs. Make 'em real fat, it will."

"Damn-to-hell, woman. Them hogs can eat pumpkins. Corn's too good to feed hogs."

"We can use some corn for our own selves. You ever think of that?" she say then, looking down on him. Mama was a big woman. She stood several inches taller than Papa. Papa, he be like me when I got growed up—a little-bitty fart—no bigger than a scrawny banty-rooster.

"I don't like corn. Sides, when I sell all my corn liquor, we be cash-fat. We can *buy* what corn we need to eat."

Mama would always say that there wudn't no need to talk to him about it after that. But she always would every year anyhow even if it do no good. Every fall he always made all of our corn crop into whiskey and sell it to the white people in the towns for several parishes around. Especially in Alexandria.

8

Now, he could shore make good corn whiskey. I can still hear that conversation and other ones like it. Fact, he taught me how to make whiskey so that when I got to be a growed man, I was figgered to be the best whiskey maker around our parts. I don't intend to brag none, but hell, a fact *is* a fact. Whiskey making was to become plenty times my economic standby and salvation, and—to tell the whole truth, too, brother—my wreck and ruination. But that's another part of my story.

Like I said, they was seven of us younguns in the family, and Grandpapa Arceneaux lived with us, too. Grandpapa was head medicine man and our chief, but while I was still a little-bitty feller, he got so stove-up with rheumatism and arthritis that he give up being active at that kind of work. You might think he could of doctored hisself for them ailments, but jist like in the white world, an Indian doctor what gits sick is always his own worst patient. My mama, who learned everything, or near-bout as much as she could, from Grandpapa, become the medicine maker for all us and, jist like Grandpapa had did, she doctored Tunica and Biloxi people plenty of times, too.

They was a lot more Tunicas than us, maybe eighty, ninety folks or so, and they had they own chief. Actually, they was many more of them folks in they tribe, but they lived off over at Baton Rouge or New Orleans and hardly come around any. They was three, four Biloxi families in the area, too, but since they didn't talk any Indian language at all anymore, we lumped them in with Tunicas. Now most of the Tunicas couldn't talk they Indian language neither. Maybe a handful or so could, but most couldn't. We Ofos talked a whole different language, and we sort of kept by usself as a separate tribe, even if we did have a lot of cousins who was with them and who considered theyself as Tunicas or Biloxis. I heared it said, by Dr. William Allerton Payne hisself, the noted authority on all us around Sherrillton, that the Biloxi language, before it died out, was close to Ofo. And he was right, I know, since a wise old Ofo—my grandpapa—told me it was so.

Our tribe was always little. The story goes we had always been kicked around by them real bigger ones—the Choctaws, Chickasaws, Quapaws. Maybe it was because of this very littleness that we tended to isolate usself from all other folks, Indians as well as whites. Even though they wudn't that many Indians in our part of Louisiana when I was little, we kind of jist stayed to usself. We got along pretty good with everybody—the white people, who was mostly Cajuns, the niggers, as well as other Indians—but we sort of knowed that we had to have some things that was our own private business and that was particular to ourownselfs, and so it be.

In Ofo Town—which is what we called our little quarter of houses and cabins and cotton patches that we had off to ourownselfs—we growed up learning real quick how to deal with white folks. We knowed that with a lot of them you never knowed from one second to the next that they might knock your head off, so we was taught to be real quiet and silent around them. Not stuck-up or anything like that, you understand, but jist be quiet till you knowed for shore what kind of person you be dealing with. We was taught, all us Ofo and Tunica and Biloxi kids—and I spect the same is true for Choctaws and Navajos or all other Indian folks—to not look directly in the eyes of white men you never knowed. No telling what-all kind of meanness you might stir up by looking such people in the eye. And since we was taught, above all things, to be respectful to everybody, and everything, around us, and ourself, too, why, this was one of our main ways of showing respect—by not staring at a stranger's face and eyes. Later on, and I still find it kind of puzzling, I heared some white people say that that Indian way of not looking you in the eyes was jist the opposite of what I say here now. I don't agree with them authorities on Indian people, but I spect my opinion don't amount to a pile of bird shit to them no-how.

Anyways, they's a story handed down to us from a long time back there about one of the Tunica headmen and what happened to him when he was dealing with white people. The chief, a man name Melacon, ast a Cajun man name Moreau not to set up a fence across our land. When Moreau refused Melacon's request, Melacon then taken out all the fence posts. That Moreau then taken out his pistol and point-blank shot Chief Melacon in the head and killed him. Moreau was never tried for murder, never spent a day in jail, and he kept the land. And it's still kept by some of his offsprings today.

Now I tell this story about Chief Melacon, and these things about dealings with white folks, not to upset white folks or jist to drag up old things from way back. It ain't my intention to go out of my way and deliberate-like slur any white person—cause for one thing I have had a lot of white friends in my time—one I even figger saved my life in the war—but I jist want to make clear about what me and the other Indian younguns of my time had to learn when we was growing up. We had to learn to deal with white people in ways that, more than anything else, would help us to save our lives. Some white people looked down on us and expected us to scamper out of they way or git knocked a-flying, and others treated us fair in a person-to-person way. You jist never knowed what to expect from one to the next, and you had to learn how to make do with each one you meet.

Another reason I tell that story about Chief Melacon is to point out something about our land and our feeling we have as Indian tribes. None of us in the State of Louisiana—Ofos, Tunicas, Biloxis, Houmas, Chitimachas, Atakapas, Choctaws—had treaty relationships with the U.S. government, and they was only the flimsiest agreements with the State of Louisiana. Fact is, I never knowed what a treaty was till I met Indians from Oklahoma and New Mexico and other places out west. Without no treaty, I found out, we wudn't considered Indians by the government, and because of that we couldn't go to them fancy Indian health clinics that I later learned about. And we couldn't git schooling through the BIA. And, hell-fire, that BIA is something else I growed up not knowing a thing about. I spect as far as the U.S. government and the State of Louisiana was concerned we was all gone—or that we was all vanished, which was the word used that I have heared a lot about over the years.

But in them days we never thought of ourself as a vanishing people. Except probly for one time. I spect I was about ten then. I remember Mama and Papa talking about some Indian man out in California that had jist died and who was sposed to be the last person of his tribe. How he had got famous for being that and how he had lived in one of them museums and all. Hearing Papa read about it out loud from the newspaper, that sounded near-about like the end of everything. I remember Papa got a faraway thoughtful look on his face and said, "Well, pretty soon all us Indians gonna be gone. This ain't our world no more." It was hard for any of us to spute his word, so we all jist changed the subject, started talking about our mink traps or something like that.

2

Jist Doing What's Handy

I can remember what the early mornings in the fall used to be
like. All us kids had to miss out of school, picking cotton for
the first eight or ten weeks of the school term. We couldn't go to
the white kid school or even the nigger school. Our school only
happen ever once in a while, depending on who got sent out our
way to do it. The few years we had a school it was mostly like
this: We'd go down and enroll around the first day of September
and go to school that one day, and then you wouldn't see hide or
hair of us at that school until way up in November, right after the
time of the first big deer hunt by state law was and after all the
cotton was got in. Then we all come back to school.

I remember one particular old lady with a big crooked nose
who was my first-grade teacher—she used to look real-mean at
me, with that bent-outa-shape nose and them wire-framed glasses
and that splotchy white face, and I'd have real bad nightmares a
lot of nights. I don't know why, but she sho use to scare the living
daylights out of me. She beat my butt for jist about everything,
but mostly, I guess, for things I deserved to get a paddling for. But

not always. One time, she whupped me for something another kid done after some other kids told on me. Claimed I done something when I didn't. Actually, what happened was this mostly-white kid name PeeWee pushed another little snot-nose in the bayou, and then him and his friends told Old Lady Mitchell—that was the teacher's name—that I done it. Course, I denied it, but it never done me a lick of good. She marched me off into that little cloakroom that was off to the side of the first-grade room, and she whupped my butt with a pine-wood paddle to the tune of "The Star-Spangled Banner." I was sore for days. Well, after that, Old Lady Mitchell had my number. She found all kind of occasions to whup me and soon the word got to be going around that I was a bad kid. Was I jist to look cross-eyed or something, then *BAM!* she taken me off into the cloakroom and paddle my butt. Got to where I hated school. Especially the first grade. And when we Indian kids run into Cajun and other white kids, they would make fun of me and my brothers and sisters and cousins for talking Indian. Like our parents had done, we had to learn English real quick jist so them mean-ass white kids wouldn't make fun of us. It was sho hard, but we done it.

Naturally, all us Indian kids usually failed the first grade and had to repeat it. I wudn't no exception. I had Old Lady Mitchell for a teacher again, and she still made my schooltime miserable for me. Got so I hated that old heifer. I played hooky ever chance I got, and that got me into trouble, too. I couldn't win for losing. Finally, though, I made it out of the first grade. Jist as well, too, cause if I'd stayed there another year, I'd of outgrowed the chairs.

Second and third grades was better. I learned to do my lessons, read about Alice and Jerry and Spot. I learned to keep my mouth shut and to try and not be seen. I had good teachers, ladies who didn't pick on me. My second-grade teacher was Miss Betty Lou Breaux and she was young and pretty and nice as pie to all us kids. Miss Emily Dusheyne was my third-grade teacher, and she was good, too. I begin to think that school wudn't so bad after all. And then I went into the fourth grade. First day of school in the fourth grade, I walk into the classroom, and guess who the teacher was? Yep, it was Old Lady Mitchell. She'd been switched from teaching first-graders and was now sposed to teach the fourth and fifth grades, which they put into one classroom.

Well, we taken up our dislike of each other again. And after a few whuppings, I decided to talk to Mama about it. I'd been working after school and on Saturdays with Papa in the bayous, cutting cypress timber and trapping some, and I was making my own spending-money, which I mostly spent on .22 shells and mushrat traps. Mama never liked the way Old Lady Mitchell whupped me neither, so she agreed I could stay out of school for a while. Well, that was the end of my schooling, cause I started working all the time then, making my own way, and I never did go back to school. The school people didn't give a damn if us Indian kids went or not, so they was never any fuss about me quitting. Fact, I believe they was relieved to see me quit, jist like they was when any Indian kid quit.

I was eleven year old and making my own money, was even helping out the family some, and I begin to think of myself as near-bout a man. Why, I picked cotton, drove mule teams, helped git in our other crops. I fished and sold my catch in Sherrillton, I cut timber in the bayous, gathered Spanish moss and dried it out and sold it for packing material. And, naturally, I helped Papa make whiskey. You know how it be, jist doing what's handy. And, all at the same time, Grandpapa was teaching me medicine

15

things—how to cure snake-bites, how to set broke arms, to know all about dreams and signs and other Indian kind of things like that. It had been decided a long time ago that Baptiste Junior would be our main medicine-maker when he growed up and took over from Mama and Grandpapa, but Grandpapa figured it wouldn't hurt Andrew and me none to learn something about it, too. I could read the Alexandria newspaper and the *Picayune* out of New Orleans, and I could figure out the days on the calendar, so I still made use of my schooling and so that part never went to waste. But they was no question about it. With all that I was busy doing after I quit school, I never had no real use for school no more, jist like it never had no use for me. I was going to different kind of school, was all. The School of Hard Knocks.

My three older brothers went through jist about the same mess I went through about school, only different in the way that they ended up gitting even less learning than I got. Anyway you look at it, all our years of schoolhouse learning put together didn't stack up to the years of a eight-year-old boy. But Leland and Andrew and Baptiste Junior was already used to hard work by the time I come on. They each had they own gift. Leland, tallish and skinny, was jist about the best trapper around. Ever year, he bring in coonhides a-plenty, and always lots of mink, mushrat, possum. I believe, if he ever taken it in his head to do it, he could sing charms that would make minks and coons and such to skin theyselves jist for him. Andrew, now, was the biggest of us, jist slightly less tall than Leland, but big and stout, and could he run— whooeeee! He could—and this ain't no lie—take out after a deer, after he doctored hisself up with herbs to git shet of his human smell, and flat run that deer down. In the last couple years of his life, before he went into the Army, he probly never used a gun a-tall in his hunting. Nothing but jist his feet. Now Baptiste Junior, who was jist three year older than me, was a real whiz with dealing with people. He started medicine training real early, so he knowed all about people's ways of dreaming, of how they git in bad ways for not doing the things they expected to do, how to find and keep your balance in the day-to-day. So it oughten be surprising to know that he was also a first-class businessman. I know that as first-hand fact cause we worked as partners together for a time.

My older twin sisters, Martha and Marie, was kind of backward. They was also deaf and dumb, but we all had a kind of sign language we done with them so they wudn't left out of anything. They could work at most any task if you be real careful and explain and show them jist what they's sposed to do. They done some cooking for Mama, but mostly they cleaned up and washed clothes. Looking back, I never recall seeing neither one of them in a real temper fit. Sho, they git irritated with hot weather, or being tired out, or sick, and then they might whimper or even yell. But, all in all, they was the even-temperedest ones of us all.

My little sister Camille growed up to be a real heart-stopper. Pretty, pretty—jist like Sally, the woman who become my wife— except, and I hate to say it, Camille knowed how to work while Sally wouldn't hit a lick at a snake. And Camille's little girl, Suzette, now gone, too. All three of them, though, I look back now—lost, lost. Oh, baby girls. . . .

But now I come back to them that made me and taught me the most—Mama, Papa, and Grandpapa. All three, but specially Mama and Grandpapa, taught me the ways of being a Ofo. A Indian person jist ain't born a Indian—like a Ofo, or a Tunica, or a

17

Choctaw—and let it go at that. That person need to learn to be a Ofo, or a Tunica, and such-like, and it is that learning makes them Ofos and such-like. It's learning comes through the community, even if it's jist a tiny community of three older folks or so, like ours was. We are born, we grow, and we learn—first, that we are in the Ofo world, a place made the good place it is by Sun Father, and the ground we walk on is our Mother. We have to do things right, keep everything on a even keel, don't rock the foundations, do our part to keep the world we live in and on in a good balance with the sky world above and the underworld below. Everything about being Ofo begins with this sense of evenness.

Mama first begin to teach me and Baptiste Junior how to use the plants around us—first, know all of them in every place, then to learn how and when to use them for ailments and such. Next, the stories about the plants and the world they live in. Then, how the Ofo world come about through the goodness of Sun Father and Mother Ground, then how to doctor people afflicted in they bodies and minds and dreams, and on to several other stages. It taken me years to learn all this kind of knowing. Like I told Dr. Matthew B. Smight one time: You jist can't learn it all on a weekend.

Later on, Grandpapa begin to show me things—specially how to balance out. Not only for youself, but for all your close ones, blood and not blood. All this is connected with the land we live on—the cornfields, the garden patches, the bayous and rivers, our houses, the old mounds, the sky, the Sun, and then the ceme- teries and dance grounds. I learned Corn Dance songs real young, medicine and hunting songs a little later on, and I bet a ten-dollar bill that up to fifteen minutes before they put me back in Mother Ground I still be learning something new.

So now maybe you can see that I might have said so long to Old Lady Mitchell and her pine-wood paddle, but I really never said no good-byes to learning and knowing. They's a lot to be said for the School of Hard Knocks.

And they was, on top of everything else, that damn old railroad track what run close by. It had a reputation all my living days and even way before I was born of being a real people-killer. The number of our people that has died on that damn thing would make a whole cemetery by itself. Long time ago, a chief's brother and as stout a warrior as you ever see, so I heared tell, was found dead on the tracks all cut up in a lot of parts. And not long after that, that man's sister, a medicine woman name Arsene, got hit by a train and killed, too. The Texas and Pacific Railway Company, it was called, but the Runover and Kill Company it was called, too. And then, they was my own family and how they all git wiped out by a train—but I'm gitting ahead of my story. Only Sun Father knows the honest real count of how many of us Ofos and Tunicas and Biloxis got sacrificed on them tracks—and a whole bunch of mules and cows and horses and dogs, too. I spect—no, I *know*— they all had they lives and they cared about them.

About a year after I started working, Papa decided to take us all on a long trip up into northern Louisiana and southern Arkansas. He wanted to take a load of whiskey up there to sell, he say, and he also wanted to visit an old friend of his. Papa had worked with a Quapaw man, Old Man Jack Darrysaw, in a logging camp in the river-bottom country of West Carroll Parish a long time before all us kids was born. Old Man Jack and Papa had been the only Indians in that two-camp settlement in the middle of a big cypress

swamp jist a mile or so from the Mississippi. I say two-camp cause
that's what it was: niggers on one side and white men on the
other. Papa and Jack, by agreement, stayed off by theyselves.

Anyways, Old Man Jack Darrysaw lived in Five Points,
Arkansas, where he farmed cotton, fished, and trapped—jist like
us. He had a whole passel of nieces and nephews that was name
Lawson and Thompson and I guess they made up for all the
younguns he never have hisself. They was all part Quapaw and
Choctaw—and French and Scotch, like a lot of the white people
in that part of Arkansas. You was Indian, depending on who you
talked to, or you wudn't, depending on who you talked to. Some
of them Lawson kids was red-headed as all-git-out, but they
thought Indian. They was all a hard-drinking and tough ass-
kicking bunch, and all of them meaner than a two-headed snake.
I remember one time when two of them big red-headed Lawson
boys got into a fistfight over a shoat, and one of them near-bout
bit the other'n's ear off. They was mean, them old boys was.

Well, we all left Sherrillton early one morning in July, in three
cars, and we traveled almost all morning to Lake Providence. Papa
sold most of his whiskey to some white people he knowed there,
and then we drove on up to Five Points, in Arkansas, in the south-
east part of the state. Old Man Jack lived about ten mile out of
Five Points and thirty-something from the Mississippi, and when
we got there everybody was real glad to see each other. That
same evening we all got in three mule-drawed wagons and went
over to the river and pitched tarpaulin tents on the sandbar. Papa
and Old Man Jack got a bunch of us boys take a paddle-boat and
go out in the river to set out trotlines. Pretty soon we went back
out and run the lines and got some great-big channel cats. We
stayed up way late that night, stuffing ourselfs with catfish and

cornbread and drinking coffee and corn whiskey, all getting to know each another real good. We sho had a real good time.

We stayed over on the river for three or four days, gorging ourselfs and jist plain having a big old time. Papa and Old Man Jack told stories about the logging camp in north Louisiana, and a whole bunch of hunting stories. Them old Arkansas boys sho had a lot of stories about deer hunting and hog hunting. Watt Lawson, the oldest of them boys, could tell stories by the hour about bringing down twelve-point bucks with jist a .22 rifle. And he wudn't jist swapping lies, neither, as I'm fixing to show.

When we'd been on the river about two days, I guess, Watt and his cousin Jed Thompson asked Andrew and me to go out in the woods with them to get a deer. It was summer and out of season to hunt deer, according to Arkansas law. Andrew mentioned that to Watt and he jist sneered and said something about white man's law. "Shoot!" he said, "You ever watch white men hunt? They shoot any damn thing that moves. They don't know the difference between killing bucks and killing does. They jist as soon kill a doe carrying an unborn fawn as to kill a ten-point buck. *We* don't do that. We only kill bucks. We have our own law. Hell with shikepoke law."

We went on back into the woods about a mile or so from the river. We come up on a salt-log that Watt had made a time before and we set down on the ground away from each other in different places about fifty yards apart and waited for a big buck to come up to the log. It was hot and green—green all around and so growed up with weeds and little trees and bushes that we couldn't see all that good. Locusts and other bugs made a lot of racket. Skeeters was real thick, but we kept real still and jist let them eat on us, not wanting to spook a deer, and they biting

21

wudn't all that bad since that deer medicine we had on also kept most of them away. One good thing, though, was it was too hot in the midday sun for cottonmouths to be out.

We didn't have long to wait. Me, I didn't have no gun, but Andrew had a .410 with him, old Watt had what he called his old "True-Blue .22," and Jed had some kind of short little gun, but I don't remember now what kind, and he went off down the woods a ways from us. I jist got a scant look at that big pretty white-chested buck when he walked up to that salt-log, his head all reared back like he was King of the Woods, when Watt's .22 cracked a shot. That buck reared up on his hind legs, like a bucking stallion, and started to run when that .22 cracked again, and he fell hard to the ground with a crash. Watt'd got him twice right behind the shoulder, dead center in the heart.

We run up to him while he was still kicking. Real quick-like, Watt grabbed the antlers from behind in one hand, and with a great-big butcher knife in the other, he slit the deer's throat, all in one motion, like. Then him and Andrew hung the buck up in a hackberry and we commence to dress it out.

"Real nice one, ain't he?" Watt said while he worked real fast with his knife. He cut the liver out and divided it into three parts, giving Andrew and me a slice and keep one for hisself. We eat it raw, standing there in the hot sun, sweat and blood dripping off of our hands and forearms. Skeeters buzzed around us like little-bitty single-engine crop-duster planes. Then we got busy and finished dressing out the buck. It was a big one, all right, an eight-pointer.

We was standing there, chomping on that meat and slurping up blood, when all of a sudden two white guys come up on us. We had been so intent on that deer that we never heared them a-tall till they was almost up to us, about fifty feet away. Watt kind of backed up so that he was standing in front of the deer, like he was trying to hide it.

"Wrong time of the year to be shootin' deer, ain't it?" one of them said. He was carrying a fishing pole, but he had a pistol strapped to his side. The other man was tall and blond-headed and was carrying a pump-gun. The one what spoke was short, with a face covered over with about a week's worth of gray-brown beard stubble.

"Who's shootin' deer? We jist decided to kill one of our dogs," Watt said, still standing in front of the deer.

"That ain't no dog. Looks like a deer to me, even if I can't see his horns," the feller with the face hair said.

"You Indians jist shoot a deer whenever you damn-well take a notion, don't you?" the other man, the one with the shotgun, said.

"Yeah, we Indians alright," Watt said. "But you got it wrong. We done killed a dog."

"Yeah, we having us an Indian ceremony," Andrew spoke up now. "That why we drinking the blood like we do."

The two white fellers kind of looked at each other, and then begin ambling up to us, real slow-like.

"I think I'll take a look at that dog myself," the short guy said. "Jist to make sure it is a dog."

"Yeah, we want to make sure you ain't killed a white man's dog," the tall one said, and he laughed.

About that time Jed Thompson walked up behind us, holding his odd-looking little gun up but not actually aiming it at them.

"That dog belongs to them fellers," he said. "They ain't lying."

The two white men stopped still and while they did Jed sort of jist casual-like pointed his gun at them. He wudn't aiming directly at them, but it was close enough to the real thing. They got the message. In the meantime, Andrew real casual-like picked up his gun. I was wishing I had one. Watt was still standing in front of the deer.

"Well, you boys take it easy, now, you hear?" The short feller said, and he and the other one turned around and hurried on back into the woods. We waited a minute or so, listening, but no more sound of them could be heard.

"Let's get on out of here," Watt said. From then on I knowed they was always the danger of what some white men would do to us if they was to have they way about it. I learned something about staying on my guard when I was around them. We slung the deer on a pole and hustled on back to the river. We had to take turns carrying him, with the odd man carrying the tin lard bucket full of guts that we planned to cook up for the dogs.

Everybody was real glad to have some fresh deer meat. That night Watt told the story about the men several times. Old Man Jack said he thought he knowed who them two fellers was, and if it was who he thought, then they wudn't likely to tell the law on us. What they would likely do, he said, would be to take the deer away from us at gunpoint. But to be on the safe side, Watt cut off the deer's head and throwed it in the river, horns and all.

We stayed over on the river for a couple more days and then went back to the Darrysaw farm, where all us Darkos pitched in to help the Lawson clan cut they hay and round up some of they hogs that was running loose in the woods. That was the afternoon them two Lawson boys, Lester and Chester, got in a fight over the shoat, each one of them claiming that it belonged to him. Old Man Jack and Watt tried to break them up at first, but after a while Old Man Jack laughed and said, "Hell, let them fight it out. Maybe them two big hunks will kill each other off and save me the misery of having to worrying about them all the time." And that's what we done—we jist let them fight on till one of them near-bout bit the other'n's ear off. I don't know which one done the biting since I never could keep them straight, they looked so much alike.

Well, anyway, pretty soon it come time for us to leave. It was a real good visit, but I for one was sort of anxious to get back home again. I'd left a pretty good job toting cypress knees over to Alexandria to a feller that made lamp-stands out of them. He contracted me to haul them in for him and he was a real genu-wine piss-ant to work for. He slaved my butt off, like he thought physical labor was in danger of going out of style and it was up to him all by hisself to make sure it never. But he paid good—at least, it be better than what I got as a swamper for the Sherrillton tannery, or what I made part-time selling hides or whiskey, which was always on-again, off-again. Of course, the whiskey and the hides was jist side things—extry cash to help out in the slack times—cause despite it being wartime, it was still the slack time for us in Louisiana. This was all some years before they started the build-up of all them big army camps that you find all over the state nowadays.

3

New Iberia

Time went on by. For several years off and on I worked for
Zeringue, the Cajun man that bought cypress knees to make
lamps out of. I even helped him start his own lumber business,
too. Then I quit and taken a job as a roustabout way down around
New Iberia. Working down there was the first time I ever been
away from home by myownself. It was hard work. I put in twelve,
fourteen hours a day, but bring in good money. Even got myself a
tin lizzie after a time.

Things wudn't going too good at home. I would like to of
stayed home, but it got so the money I made in the oil fields was
needed by them at home more than ever before. Several things
happened that was a real setback for all us. My brother Andrew
was drafted by the army in 1917, and he died of the flu the next
year in a army camp somewhere up in New Jersey, without ever
even getting overseas. They sent his body back home and we buried him down by the bayou, close to my grandmama's grave, in
the place where Darkos been buried for ages. Then, in the springtime after the war ended, Papa had a stroke and he was crippled

all up on his whole right side. He wudn't never the same again cause it afflicted his way of talking and thinking, as well as him not being able to walk good anymore. Then, to make bad matters even worse, a white man name Farrell killed my oldest brother, Leland, in a knife fight over at Bunkie. We buried him out by Andrew, and the law never done a blame thing to that white man.

All these troubles seem to happen real fast-like, one right after the other one. We all didn't have time to git over one bad time in a proper way when the next one happened. One right after the other. It's like people say around here: trouble is like muscadines— it comes in bunches. Andrew, that was the best deer-hunter around, and probly the fastest Ofo that ever burned up a trail, was I guess the one I was closest to. If after all these years I ain't any better hunter and fisherman than I be—and I do git along at it passably well—then I know the reason I ain't is cause Andrew left us too young and never had the time to show me all the right things to do. And old Leland, that big fun-loving oldest brother of mine, he left too soon, too, and never had time to teach me how to have a good time in the easy kind of way. With me, since I never learned it right, I always went too hard after fun—at least in that time of my life when I was sort of out of touch with the Ofo ground. I still git sad sometimes when I think of them two teacher-brothers of mine and I know for a fact my life would have been a better road for me if I had them old boys around me for a lot longer time.

My brothers dying off hurt Papa real hard. He used to set in the front room or out under the shade tree in the yard and cry, real easy-like, like a little girl. It got so I had to git away from him, cause I couldn't stand that whimpering cry of his. I still think about it now and then, and it always hurts me a lot to remember how Papa spent his last years kind of like a mashed bug. Like something that had its back broke, too, and some of its limbs but still lived. He could still git around a little bit, but he act like he was lost and confused most of the time.

Grandpapa, he was also pretty poorly at that time. He was near-bout seventy-five and stove-up with all them crippling arthritis afflictions, and he act like he was jist counting his remaining days, too—like Papa seemed to do. They was father-in-law and son-in-law, but to us in the family they look near-about like they was twins.

It was sometime toward the end of all our family troubles that I struck up an acquaintance with a little old gal name Sally Fachette. It was in New Iberia. She worked in town at The Four-Leaf Clover Cafe as a waitress. She was Houma Indian and come from Bayou Cane, which was about eighty mile down the road in Terrebonne Parish. She was prettier than a summertime butterfly, and for me—well, it was like them *True Romance* stories tell about: love at first sight. I would of waded through ten mile of swampwater for jist one little old kiss—she was that sweet and pretty. She was little, jist a dab over five foot tall, and her reddish-black hair was fancy-bobbed like the white women done theys at the time, but that never put me off none. I liked that style. But I like long hair on a woman, too. I ain't particular. Me, I can take all kind of style.

I used to finish up my evening shift down at the oil rig, be tired as the daylights but too dumb to know it, yet I'd head on down to that cafe, and there she be, all prettier than a Kodak picture and smelling sweeter than a lily-pad. I'd be like the other fellers there, straight offen work and dirty as a rooting hog. After a time or two, though, I noticed she wudn't paying me no more

attention than a scratching skunk would pay a stinkbug. Even if I
was Indian, jist like her. But I never give up. I set there for about a
week, watching her flirt up to all them Cajuns and other white
fellers, treating life like she didn't have no tomorrows, and I'd be
setting over by the jukebox, drinking too much beer and breaking
up inside like a clod of gumbo in a puddle of water. Of course,
them other fellers had the advantage of me, probly cause I *was*
Indian like her. I started to figure that maybe she made up her
mind a long time ago not to tie herself down with no Indian, that
maybe she figured an Indian man couldn't give her things like a
white man could. I knowed some of the gals back home who
thought that way. And when I thought that, why it made me
even more determined than ever before: I wudn't going to give
up without no try. But for a while that consoling thought give me
no comfort since she still wudn't paying me no attention. Them
guys would flirt back at her and she'd jist shine, it look like, and
come closing time she'd have her pick of the lot and would head
on out honky-tonking with Jerry or Mike or Etienne or whoever.
Her pick. Sho as hell not mine. Scraping the bottom of the trough
was more like it to me, she was.

Anyway, she was going out ever night, kicking up her heels,
and I was getting sadder by the day. One night I decided to talk to
her. She come by my table after waiting on somebody else who
was setting close to me. I said, "Hey, taique. Where you from?"

First off, I knowed she wudn't no Ofo, since they was so few
of us and I knowed them all. And I knowed she wudn't no other
kind a Sherrillton Indian since I knowed all our own folks, and as
I said before, we wudn't too many, so I called her the Choctaw
word for young lady. Now I don't know Choctaw to talk it, but I

do know a word or two. Choctaw had always been kind of the talk near-bout every Indian in my part of the South could talk at least a few words of. I knowed most of the Tunicas and Biloxis, too, so I figured she wudn't one of them. That left the Chitimachas, and they was sort of like us Ofos and Tunicas since they didn't have much of they language left, and also the Houmas and Choctaws, who jist about was the same people, language-wise.

"You talking to me?" she said in jist regular old cotton-patch English, and she wudn't flirting or grinning none a-tall. I guess I made a tilt—like on them slot machines, how you tilt and the game ends, if you know what I mean?—and she looked at me real cool-like.

"I did," I said. "I ast you where you from."

She looked at me, then at my greasy britches and at my dirty fingernails, and then she say, pretty smart-alecky, "What's it *to* you, buster?"

"Aw, don't be like that," I said, "I jist wondered where you was from. You remind me of back home." I must of sounded sad to her cause she stood there looking at me, holding the beer tray against her hip. Now that I think about it, I must of sounded downright whiney, but at least it look like it might of had some effect cause she had stopped and stood there.

"If you really want to know, I'm from Bayou Cane," she said then and said it in the Cajun way.

"Bayou Cane, huh? That's in Terrebonne Parish, ain't it," I said. Now I knowed good and well Bayou Cane was in Terrebonne Parish, but I had got her to talk to me at least. Then I said, "What kind of Indian you are?" thinking as I asked her that she might git mad since a lot of Indians in the South, especially in

Louisiana, don't like to be taken for Indian out in public. They want to be taken for French or I-talian, or something like that. At least that's what Mama told me one time.

But it didn't seem to faze her none. She looked at me, and then she grinned for the first time and I felt my heart did a skip and a jump. She said, sweet as corn-syrup pie, "I am French. But my grandpere, he is Houma." Then she was gone, headed over to the bar to fill up her tray with beer bottles. Hell, she wudn't no more French than I be a blue-tick hound. She was Houma—period.

Well, my hopes went up then. I hung around there all night till closing time, waiting to see if maybe I might get a chance to invite her to go with me. No luck, though. She left out with a snotty-looking white jasper that was all decked out in a three-piece suit and wearing honest-to-goodness goddamned spats. And I didn't even git to talk to her no more neither.

I decided to stay away for a few days, jist to see if I could, but mainly to try to shake that spell it look like she had put over on me. I commenced to spend my nights staying in my room in the rooming house, or setting on the screened-in front porch with some of the older roomers, listening to the radio. But, you know, when you in your twenties you can only take jist so much of *Amos and Andy* and hillbilly music that you can't dance to set-ting on a porch. I'd set there trying to follow all the rigamarole old Kingfish was going through, or sometimes I'd jist set in my room staring at the wall paper. Other times, on the front porch with the old folks a-rocking away in they rockers, I'd have to act like I was at least half-interested in what Old Lady Marchand or one of them others was insisting on gossiping about some other roomer—somebody else who jist happened at the time to be away from that courthouse being held ever night on the porch—and I tell you, I was about to climb the walls.

The landlady, Miss DuClos, would chase us all off of the porch at nine o'clock, and she shut the radio off and I'd be thinking that in an hour The Four-Leaf Clover would close and *she* would be stepping out with some fancy-pants, while I—and then it dawned on me. I'd git me some fancy duds, too. I'd damn-well outshine all them cake-eaters! I still had two days left before I'd intended on going back to The Four-Leaf Clover, and while I was gitting ready to go to bed I decided that the next afternoon I'd go git me a new suit and a tie and a hat and a new pair of shoes that'd be so shiny and black that they'd put a wet watermelon seed to shame.

And that's what I done. I had saved me up quite a bit of money, even if I was giving Mama and them most of what I made ever week. I went to the fanciest clothes store in New Iberia and I bought me a three-piece suit. The britches, coat, and vest all matched and was gray as a shikepoke egg, but with real light yellow stripes running throughout. I got a bowler hat, gray, too, and a darker shade than the suit clothes, but with no yellow stripes on it. I got a pair of black patent-leather shoes, too. But no goddamn spats. I wudn't gonna go that far. That night I tried on my suit in the privacy of my room and I was pleased to see it all fit me like a top. I looked at myself in the mirror over the chest-of-drawers: I was the best-dressed Ofo on the block, I want you to believe it.

Well, I planned my plan then. My suit was ready, I had a good-working car, had money enough. I looked in the mirror again and sized up my face. I never been in what you might call the handsome category, so there was nothing I could do about that. But I could at least git my hair cut some. I knowed of a nig-ger barbershop around the corner from the rooming house that usually stayed open till midnight, so I went down there and got them to lower my ears a bit. Back in my room, I started in on my hands, washing them again and again, first in some gasoline and then in soapy water, and I even taken my toothbrush to git the grease and grit out from under the fingernails.

Next day after work I went straight back to my room, again with no idea at all of stopping at The Four-Leaf Clover. I eat at the rooming house with the other boarders after cleaning up some, then as the night wore on I went back to my room and decked myself out like a dandy.

Well, sir, when I showed up at The Four-Leaf Clover around nine you could see all them regulars' eyes kind of bug out at me, but I never paid them no attention. I looked around, but I didn't see her nowhere. *What if she ain't here?* I thought, and jist as I was about to ask the bartender where she was she come out of one of the backrooms carrying a trayload of hamburgers. She seen me and nearly stopped, but she didn't. Jist paused, and looked at me and hurried on with the order she had.

I waited for her to wait on me. Directly, she come over with her tray on her hip.

"Well," she says. "Ain't you all dressed up? Where you been keeping yourself?"

"This?" I said, real cool-like, and looking down at my duds and waving my hand a little. "Nothing out the ordinary. Where I been?" And here I started in fibbing. "I been home," I said. "Had to go home to take care of a business deal."

"I wouldn't of thought you was in business," she says. "I taken you for a roustabout."

"Well," I said, "I do work at that some, but I have me a business, too. And it takes up a lot of my time. Keep me on the run." Now I no more owned a business than Huey P. Long made president, but damn-to-hell, I had her attention, and I was doing my best to keep it.

"Well, my, my," she say. "Who'd a-thought? It just goes to show you, appearances ain't what they seem to be."

"Why don't you let me take you out tonight, I'll tell you all about it." Now brains I might not have much of, but gumption I got.

"I don't know. I kind of promised Mr. Tyler I'd go dancing with him, but—"

"No buts," I say. "You and me, *we'll* go dancing, and afterwards I'll take you for a spin in my new Ford. You can show me the sights around here." Then I leaned closer to her, hoping the lights in the place would glitter in all that pomade and Vaseline I had gobbed on my hair, and I say, real private-like, "I even have some genu-wine Tunica White Lightning. No taste in the world like it." Now I knowed she drunk cause I seen her sometimes taken a swig out of a beer bottle now and then there in The Four-Leaf Clover when she figgered the owner wudn't looking.

"Now, where'd you git any Tunica White Lightning?" she says. "I hear that's hard to come by."

"Make it myself," I said. "Make it, and sell it. Best in the state."

"Then you Tunica? I thought you was Choctaw."

"Nope. I'm Ofo. We live close by the Tunicas."

She hadn't heard of us Ofos. Which was no surprise. Not many people have. Even a lot of other Indians around about the state. Hell, even most folks in Sherrillton, jist two mile from our land, don't know really what kind of Indian we be. I started telling her more about me, my folks, my "business," when Slim, the bartender, yelled to her, "Sally, you got customers to wait on!" and so she had to go.

Well, now, all in all, that's how I started in on a lot of things. That night was my turning point in more ways than one. To this day I never stopped being amazed at how so many things can all of a sudden come on you, things you hadn't planned on or expected at all, and then fore you know it your life is on a completely different road than the one you always knowed. That night—yes, I got my date with Sally, and she become my own special girlfriend and all, and we even ended up tying the knot together. Not only that, but that night was, like them *Police Gazette* magazines say, the time I embarked on my life of crime.

How did I embark, you wonder? Well, two ways, the way I see it now. First, you remember I said that I told her I had a "business"? Well, while I was waiting for her to git off work so we could go on our date together, I found I had to think up some kind of business to have, something to impress her, so I told her I was a whiskey-maker and that I had money coming in hand over fist. Now, it's true I made whiskey, but I wudn't no out-and-out businessman at it. Sold a jug now and then, was all. But when I told her that, her eyes got big as saucers. We was setting in my Ford, listening to the dance music coming out over the parking lot at the roadhouse where we was. We had already had a sample of some Tunica White Lightning and we both had a nice glow on. Anyway, I told her that fib that I was a big-ass bootlegger, and I could tell that she was impressed as all-git-out.

Well, I'd of let it go at that, but jist a little while later on while we was still setting in that parking lot listening to the dance music, that guy Tyler that she stood up for me come over to my car. He seen us and he was mad as hell. He was already drunker than a prune and so pie-eyed he couldn't hardly stand, but he come over and begin chewing Sally out.

"So you take up with this little black-assed, pint-sized piss-ant, huh? Stand me up for him, huh!" He was one of them loud-mouth drunks that liked to say "huh!" a lot at the end of his sentences. His face was so red and swole up from drinking so much, he look like one of them big mad leghorn roosters. He was a big pussel-gutted bastard and I wudn't looking forward to tangling with him none. He begin threatening us, yelling and cussing, and folks, I tell you, I was getting knock-kneed. Mind now, I never wanted to fight him, he was a whole lot bigger than me, but I made up my mind right away that I would if it come down to it. Besides, I was getting pretty mad, myownself, too. Then Sally, who was pretty mad herownself, said to him that if he didn't leave us alone, I—meaning me—was going to take out my pistol and shoot him between the eyes. Now I did have an old .22 pistol in the glove compartment, and right away while he wudn't looking I took it out and shot about four, five times straight up in the air. Well, Tyler, he like to shit his britches. He yelled out "God help me," or some such, and turned all colors and took out running like a stripedy-assed ape. Sally and me had a big laugh and I started the car and we burned a streak of rubber on the pavement leaving out of there like we done.

Well, like I said, that begin everything. Next night, going into The Four-Leaf Clover to pick Sally up, it seem that the word had got around. I had white people that never give me the time of day before treating me like I was a big shot, buying me beer and saying "Mr. Darko this" and "Mr. Darko that," and pretty soon I

37

found I had a reputation on my hands. And I'd be lying like a possum if I was to say I didn't like it. I did. And, to top it off, I even begin to run whiskey. First, I had people coming up to me in The Four-Leaf Clover and asking me to git them some, and so I actually started in doing jist that. It become downright profitable. You might remember it was Prohibition and they was a big demand for good whiskey then. It got so I had to quit my job at the oil field jist so I could meet all my obligations as a businessman.

4

Tough Guys

Now in case you don't know it, shikepokes is a wading bird that we got plenty of in Louisiana. They be several different varieties, but they all have in common that they like to wade in water, like to hang out in marshes and swamps and along bayous and rivers and lakes, which we also got a lot of in Louisiana. Another thing, too, about shikepokes is they sometimes take over other birds' nests. Jist come in and take over, like they too damn lazy to build they own. Well, sir, that's the main reason why we Indian people in Louisiana—and in Arkansas and Mississippi, too, I come to find out—call white folks shikepokes. On account of the way they come in and taken over in our country. But, you know, jist as ducks and geese and pelicans and cranes and plovers have to learn to live with the shikepokes, so did us Indian people, too, have to learn to get along with white folks. It ain't been exactly a bed of roses, but it ain't always been a all-out briar patch neither.

What I'm gitting around to saying is that up to the time I got going full-time on the bootlegging and whiskey-running, I never had much to do with white folks. Oh, sho, they was always around, in Sherrillton and later when I worked oil fields and whatnot all around Alexandria and New Iberia, but I could genly stay out of they way. But seem to me like after I taken up with Sally, and them fellers around The Four-Leaf Clover begin making a big to-do about me and my business, I could not turn around without stepping on white folks. For one thing, they was my main customers. Granted that Prohibition was one big sorry-ass shikepoke law, but it look to me like white people the main ones who was out there breaking that law in all kind of ways. Course, I broke it, too. It was a stupid law. Even now, more than thirty years later, I still say it be a stupid law. I always feel that you can't expect laws to stop people from doing what they want to do. If people want to drank, let them drank. And when dranking is bad for a person, like when he become a drunk, why, they ain't no law around going to make him sober. He gotta do that for hisself. He gotta decide to do that on his own. Can't nobody make him do no otherwise. But that is how so many shikepoke laws work— they say "Do this" or "Do that," and if you spute them, then they come back at you with "Do this cause I tell you to." And if you was to say "why?" Then they still come back with "You do this cause I tell you to." Never no reasons give why you should do things, only that you goddamned well better do it or you git your ass stomped.

Anyway, pretty soon I taken trips to New Orleans and to Shreveport, and on out to Dallas. My brother Baptiste Junior was busier than a dog with fleas back in Sherrillton, doubling and then tripling the whiskey-making so that I can have more to sell. Before I knowed it, I had three fellers working for me. They was Brady and Lester Blagg, two white fellers from out by Alexandria, and a nigger feller name Benny Stokes from New Iberia. We all got along good. The Blagg brothers, to they eternal credit, never seem to look down they noses at me or Benny. Course I's paying they salary, but I spect even if I wudn't they boss, they would of still acted decent. They was good fellers, not overly bright neither one of them, but good hard workers. Benny, now, he was smarter—fact is, it look to me like sometime he have a adding machine in his head, the way he could tote up numbers so fast. It ain't no surprise then that I tell you he become our bookkeeper.

I made a rule that I wanted the other fellers to follow. When we traveled by car, or by train, as we done sometime, we was always to be well-dressed. I spect that dolling-up I done for Sally's benefit back in our courting had rubbed off on me, and I figgered that since I was now a businessman I ought to dress up like one. Besides, the dapper look was in for high-living gentlemen in the libation supply business in them days. Lester and Brady, I told them, could wear they overalls and raggy caps while they was working or driving while on the road, but when we went to a public place in some town or city, then they was expected to wear they suits. I still couldn't go in a lot of white saloons on my own in places like Dallas or Little Rock, so I got Brady to do that for us. I would go along, like his assistant, and so I made sho he never got cheated on any cash transactions. Same thing with Benny. I let him handle the nigger nightclubs. All considered, we done pretty good.

Sally took to the high-life right off. We got married about a month after I emptied out my pistol for Mr. Tyler's benefit, got a little white house with blue trim and shutters and porch all around it right off the downtown part of New Iberia. She quit her job, we bought a radio, and as the dough come rolling in she had me buy her such things as mink coats and pearly necklaces and such. We eat in restaurants and cafes and hung out in dance halls and speakeasies. All the time, I was still making sure that Mama and them back home got a regular payment, too. But after a while, I begin to notice Sally didn't cotton too much to me giving Mama money.

"Tom, darling," she say. "You ought to consider our needs first, before you give your money away like that."

When she talk like that, it rankled me like a hobnail on a corn, but I patiently tell her that wudn't the case.

"I'm not 'giving' that money away, Sally. It's my responsibility to my family."

"Oh, I know, Tom, honey. But you gotta remember that I got needs, too."

"Well, what are you needing now?" I say, taking in the radio and clothes and fur coats and icebox and new dishes and I don't know what-all.

"Besides," I go on. "Remember that Baptiste Junior is my partner. He make the product, and I peddle it. And he got his share coming, too."

She'd keep on arguing, not loud or mean, jist sort of whiney, until I would have to funny it out of her by tickling her ribs or playing kissy-face, or more especially as time went by, taking her out to a fancy cafe or a spiffy new speakeasy.

One day in December of 1929 I got a telegram from a customer of mine in Memphis name of Weathers. Said if I could bring up double my usual product next trip up, it could really be worth my time and trouble. Course, "product" and "trip" was words that he never had to go into a lot of explaining about, and I knowed

42

what he meant. So, Lester and Brady and Benny and me headed out a couple of mornings later in two cars with hidden compartments for the stash and got into Memphis in the late afternoon. Come to find out, though, they was something else in the wind.

"Tom," Weathers said. "I couldn't tell you this in a telegram or over the telephone, but your product is being requested by another party."

"Another party? What you mean?"

"Joe Saltis, up in Chicago, has heard of you and your Tunica White Lightning, and he says he'll pay you double for whatever size shipment you bring him."

"Double?" I say. "And why to Chicago? That's a long way out of my territory."

"Well," he say. "As I hear it, it's getting to be really hard getting good whiskey in Chicago, because of the gang wars up there."

"Oh, no," I say. "I don't want no part of them gang wars. I heared how them guys up there be killing each other off by the dozens. No siree Bob, I don't want no part of that."

"I'm sorry you feel that way, Tom. I was hoping you'd say yes."

"How come? And besides, wouldn't me doing a trip up there cut into your business?"

"Well, I was hoping you'd say yes, because I'd already mentioned to Mr. Saltis that he could most likely count on you to bring him a shipment of prime drinking-stuff." Weathers had set down behind his desk while we talked in his office, which he run out of a car barn and which in them days people was beginning to call gasoline stations. He looked tired and peaked, like he been

43

running and losing too many foot-races. "And, no, you wouldn't be cutting in on me, Tom. Fact of the matter is, I'm getting out of the business."

He went on to tell me that the local law in Memphis was tightening the screws on speaks and runners. Also, that he didn't cotton too much to the Chi-Town guys—the same ones he was trying to fix me up with—and he wanted to enjoy his old age on his farm down out by the Mississippi. I ast him why he was trying to hook me up with the Chicago people if he didn't trust them.

"You're right. I don't trust them. But you're a young man, Tom, and you're feisty as hell. If there's anybody around who can hold his own with that crew of wops and micks, it's you." Then he went on, looking directly at me, "But, if I was you, I wouldn't do more than a couple of jobs of business with them. No more than a couple of runs, make a pile of dough on them, and then get shet of them."

He told me how them gangs in Chicago had divided the whole city up into territories and it seem like they spent all they waking hours trying to bump each other off. Said at least three hundred people been killed in gang wars over the past ten years and that they didn't seem to be no letup in sight. Said that a guy call Scarface was trying to claw his way up to the top of the heap. Fact is, Weathers say, it was this Scarface guy that was putting pressure on Saltis and making Saltis look outside Chicago for new whiskey and beer connections. And that's where Tom Darko come in, he say.

Well, to keep this story from gitting too long—I decided, after talking it over with Benny and Brady and Lester, to give Chicago a shot. I had a phone number for Saltis so I give him a call and say

44

we on our way. Before I could say too much, Saltis interrupt and say for us to hurry and get there. We did. We drove straight on from Memphis to Chicago, going all night and getting there mid-morning next day.

Saltis and a whole gang of gun-toting helpers met us in the back alley behind a import business warehouse. He was pale-complected Polack-man, on the fattish side, dressed real spiffy-diffy in a tuxedo with a carnation boutiniere in a lapel and whitish cream-color spats that look like pancake batter poured out on the tops of his shoes. All his muscle guys was dressed up, too, in topcoats and fedoras, and big bulges where they had they hardware hid.

We made our transaction, at the price that Mr. Weathers had told to me, and I was satisfied. More than satisfied, the fact of the matter be. It was already colder than a block of ice, and none of us old Louisiana boys had no topcoats on. And I was also anxious to get on our way, first to get to a warm hotel room and then to be back on our way to Louisiana, but mainly to git some distance between us and these decked-out pasty-faces what was carrying more hardware than a army arsenal. I wudn't comfortable around these dudes one bit. Jist as I was starting to wrap up our deal and say our so-longs, Saltis say, "Why don't you gentlemen come on inside, have a drink and warm yourselves up before you go?"

Now I wudn't partial to that idea, but I seen something odd in Saltis's fish-looking eyes and I say, "Why, thank you, sir. That be real polite of you." And we go inside, and lo and behold—that im-port warehouse was really a speakeasy, with a long goddamn bar with whiskey bottles and beer taps and such, and a bunch of gam-bling tables and slot machines. They was about a half-dozen girls hanging around, as waitresses and hat-check girls and cigarette girls. They was also a sprinkling of customers in the place, dranking they dranks and hanging around the gambling tables.

Saltis kind of look funny at Benny, and Benny, he quick-like move to the kitchen area where he seen a couple of coloreds standing around, and for a moment then Saltis look at me real close and extra-long, too, but he never said nothing. But, hell, Benny and me, we be use to that kind of shit. Me and Saltis set down at a table and a real pretty girl come over and pour us all shots of whiskey. Saltis said to our health and Lester and Brady and me did the same to him. We was jist starting to get a bit comfortable after Saltis poured us our second dranks when all of a sudden the front door of the place bust open and a big, beefy, mean-looking guy toting a Thompson submachine gun under his arm come charging right up to our table. He was backed by three other heavy-armed gunsels what was carrying they hardware in they hands and not under they camel-hair topcoats like Saltis's guys done.

"Joe," beefy guy yelled, "this is the only warning I'm giving you. I want my cut from the Waukegan haul—right now! or I'm gonna cut you down, and everybody else around here, too."

Saltis start to stand up, holding his hands, saying, "Frankie, Frankie. Let's take it easy—" but the big guy push him back into his chair.

"Now, goddamn you! You get me my money *now!*"

"Sure thing, Frankie," Saltis say, and then to one of his men standing by the bar. "Gino, come over here." You could tell that Saltis was scared as all-git-out. So was this Gino. So was all of us. Saltis spoke real soft to Gino, but where Frankie—and me—could hear, saying for him to git some money from his safe, and he give him the safe's combination numbers. In the meantime Frankie stood over us, that ugly Thompson holding us at bay like a Catahouly point a coon. He was decked out in a three-piece suit, dark brown, with a fedora to match, and had on Harold Lloyd kind of glasses. But he sho wudn't no Harold Lloyd. We set there around that table, our hands out in front of us on the table-top. He look at me then and say, real mean, "What's this black dago bastard doing here?" He's talking to Saltis, but I know he mean me.

"Oh, he's not a dago, Frankie," Saltis say. "Mr. Darko is a—" and he stop and look at me, then say, "What are you, sir?"

"I'm Indian," I say.

"Yes, Frankie. Mr. Darko is from India. He's just a customer visiting here from his home overseas."

I wudn't about to correct him, and I gave Brady the eye jist as he was about to with his two-cents. I jist hoped this mean-eyed sonofabitch would finish his business and git gone.

Then Gino come back holding a fistful of greenbacks which he started to give to Saltis, but which Frankie instead grabbed out of his hand.

"Alright now, Saltis, you cheap Polack bastard. We're quits. And from now on, it's war between us, and you can tell that scarfaced wop bastard Capone I say the same thing." Then he cut loose with that Thompson and we all dove to the floor. But he was shooting up the bar and all around, and his gunsels joined in, too. I bet they must of shot five hundred rounds. The racket—oh, my goodness. It was something else. I was jist hoping they wudn't going to lower they sights any.

They didn't. All of a sudden, they stopped shooting and run out of the place. Saltis was coming apart—crying and yelling and so forth. In between trying to git him calmed down, I look

47

around, see that nobody got hurt. Back at the kitchen area, Benny poked his head around the door. We told each other we's alright. I got Lester and Brady up off the floor, and aside from them shaking like me, they was okay, too. By now, Saltis had calmed down some.

We concluded our business and got ready to leave. I could hear some police sirens real far away but sounded like they gitting close. I say my good-bye to Saltis, and when he ast for a New Iberia phone number for me, without even thinking twice, I give him a made-up one.

Me or none of the boys cared about seeing no more of Chicago, so we started for home that same hour. Tired as we was, we genly agreed that Chicago was one damn unhealthy city. We had plenty of dough from our haul and we decided to lay low for a while—and for sho not include any more Chicago trips in our future plans.

For the next couple years I made runs jist in Louisiana and Texas, except for a time or two up to Kansas City and to Little Rock. The boys agreed with me that we never had to go to them real-big cities up north to make a good bit of change. We do pretty fine jist staying close to our home-grounds. Course, they was some drawbacks that way, too. Baptiste Junior told me that the local Sherrillton law had a warrant out for my arrest. Said the warrant go on about the Thomas Darko Gang. Now that was laying it on some thick. We was jist whiskey-makers and runners. It wudn't like none of us was bank robbers or murderers. In fact, one time Lester, he bring up the idea about us holding up a bank. He'd been hearing all that shit about people like John Dillinger and Pretty Boy Floyd and Bonnie and Clyde, and he say we oughta do something like that to let everybody know we a big bad gang, too. But I put the brakes on that hare-brained notion. I did not like stealing, if I could avoid it, and I sho as hell did not like killing, and a lot of times I even had some second thoughts about moonshining. Seem to me like most times we was running jist to be running. My folks in Sherrillton was eating pretty good the last couple years, even if it was the Big Depression and all.

But the real thing seem to be Sally. It was like no matter how much money I bring in, it wudn't nowhere near enough for her. She went through money like a rat go through cheese. Even to this day I ain't figgered out to my satisfaction where all that money went to. Sally, she buy anything that tickle her fancy. New dresses, new coats, new shoes—no matter what—something catch her eye, and zip, she got to have it. All along, she resent whatever I give to Mama and my sisters. Not only that, on occasion I give some money to Sally's own grandparents what was living in Bayou Cane, in Terrebonne Parish. Sally's mama and daddy was dead, and she been raised by her grandparents, but good land of living, she even resent them two nice old folks gitting any at all of what she considered to be *her* money. I hate to say it, but Sally was a greedy little thing. But at the time, I couldn't see it to save my hide. She say to me give her five dollar, ten dollar, fifty dollar, and I fork the stuff over. And I hate to admit it now—it was something I could not see then, but I do now—I was jist flat-out pussy-whupped. In that respect, I wudn't no different than a million other young guys around. And because of that, I stayed on that damn treadmill of making runs to Shreveport, to Dallas, to Austin, to Little Rock, working and running my butt ragged, doing things at breakneck speed. Even though I was trying to do good by my family, and by Sally, I was all in all an unevened-out person. I had no way of gitting in touch with the center of me, the way my Grandpapa had teached me, and how mama remind from time to time, "You gotta slow down, Tommy. Don't run so much, son. They gonna ketch you and th'ow you in jail, you run so much. Git off the highway and git back in the swamp for a change." All a particular Ofo and Tunica version of asting me to stop and sniff the daisies on occasion.

But a lot of other folks was doing they own treadmill thing back then, too. Around 1932, 1933, the Depression was full-force. People was out of work all over the place and men of all nations and colors was out on the highways or riding the rails looking for work, looking for a dime, looking for food, even. And they was the others running they damnedest, too, like the Darko Gang. That was when people like the Barker Gang was kicking up they heels, robbing banks right and left all over the South and Midwest. And Pretty Boy Floyd and John Dillinger and Underhill and all them. And Bonnie and Clyde. Now I knowed Bonnie and Clyde. They was trash. I apologize for speaking out-and-out bad about somebody, but they was pure trash. Real pee-drips. They would kill anybody got in they way—even they own kind. Jist a couple of thrill-happy punks, they was, with no more self-pride than a grubworm. It happen like this:

The guys and me was on our way to Austin, Texas, carrying a load of lightning. We was stopped along the side of the road, parked under some elm trees, eating baloney sandwiches, when this black Buick pull up beside us. This fox-faced skinny blond girl sticked her head out the car window and yelled, "Hey, nigger boy. You come over here."

I thought she might be talking to Benny, but no, she was

looking straight at me. And Benny, he was in the back seat of our car, kinda outa her sight. I ast if she mean me and she say, real smart-ass, "Yes, I'm talking to you, you stupid shit. Now come over here."

I was jist about to ignore her. It seem like I heared that kind of mouth-trash from people all my life and I knowed you can't do anything good talking to them. Then I seen the two men setting next to her on the front seat holding rifles or shotguns—I could not tell which—in they hands, and I decided right away I better not to do nothing to rattle them. So I walked over toward they car.

"Yessum," I say, real polite, and even push my hat back a bit as a way of tipping it. "What can I do for you?"

"Well, nigger boy," she say, in her loud whiney cottonpatch Texas voice. "You can tell us how to get back to the main road to'ards Houston."

"I beg your pardon, lady," I say, real quiet-like and still polite, looking all the time at them two jaspers holding them guns. And then I notice two more people—a man and a woman—in the backseat, but they look like they sleeping, and so I go on anyhow. "I'm not a nigger. I'm a Indian."

"Oh, git out of here, nigger boy. They ain't no more Indians around no more. Everybody knows that," she say, but she is laughing a little, and I see a snub-nose .38 laying on her lap.

"Well, you see one now," I say, and hope my words will lay right there and that she will let it alone. This young brassy shikepoke girl sho wudn't no brain surgeon—more like a damn dangerous little rattlesnake, she be. I stood there, about three foot from they car, waiting, thinking that any little old thing might set her—or them—off, so I say to myself, me, jist be calm, hear her out, try go my separate way, and hope the little heifer don't shoot me in the back. I go on, "The road to Houston be back that way, how you come, about eight mile. They's a bayou and a bridge jist before you come to the cutoff."

"Ye hear that, Clyde?" she yelled back behind her. "We done gone and missed the turn-off. I goddamn-well tole you we did! But, no. You knowed different. You stupid shit!"

The guy on the passenger side close to the door say something, but I can't make it out. Then that scrawny girl turn back to me and say, "I bet you boys know who we are, don't you?" And she look like a hungry cat looking at a sparrow, but before I could answer, she say, "Yeah. We Bonnie and Clyde. We the Barrow Gang." And kind of set there like she was expecting me to give her a reward or a A for her spelling test.

"Yes, ma'am," I say, completely in neutral. "I'm pleased to make your acquaintance."

"Goddamn! You something else, with manners and all. My, my!" Then she leaned futher out the car window and say, "I bet you really don't know who we are, do you?"

"Yes, ma'am," I say. "Seem to me like I heared you be in the banking business."

She cackled and bounced on the car seat a time or two like a two-year-old.

"Goddammit, nigger boy. You take the cake." And she cackled some more. Then she say, "Say, you boys got anything we can drank?"

Now, we had a pint bottle, about half-full, in our glove compartment, not to mention, of course, our load hid in the automobile's secret stash place.

"Why, yes, ma'am. As a matter of fact we do."

I figgered if I give them the pint bottle it might blindside them to our real stash. I turned away from her car and ast Brady to give me the bottle we had there in the glove compartment. He was trying to ast me what they was up to, but I shushed him with a quick frown and a short headshake that I hope that mean little heifer don't see. I was going back to they car when the guy on they passenger side got out and come toward me. It was the one she call Clyde. It look to me like he was already drunk. He was a short, skinny little fart, jist like me, and he had a real goofy grin on his face. He was carrying a shotgun. Look to me like a 10-gauge. "Lemme have that-there bottle, boy," he say, and I'm sho hoping he's not thinking about that gun in his hand. I give him the bottle, and he taken the cap off and glugged down about a third of it.

"Whoo-wee!" he yell when he come back up for air, and he waving that shotgun around all kind of which-way. "Lordy, lordy! That's good shine—whoo-wee!"

I jist stand there, waiting for the right time to say my excuse-me's and git us the hell out of there. Clyde, now, he was sizing me up while the other guy from they car's front seat came up beside him. This guy was nothing but a teenage kid, kind of dumb-looking.

"Where you boys headed?" Clyde ast me, but jist as I was fixing to answer I notice a little black-and-white-spotted dog come by our cars, walking in the ditch. Before I knowed it, Clyde pointed his shotgun at it, and BLAM! he blowed that dog into two or three bloody parts about ten foot away. Then him and the dumb-looking kid laugh and yell, and Bonnie joined in, too, and the kid say, "Goddamn, Clyde! I 'own see that agin! Gimme that gun!" and he taken the shotgun and blasted the biggest part of the dog's body into even littler parts. I cut my eyes over to Lester and Brady and Benny, and I could see real afraid looks on they faces. I imagine mine look the same way. Clyde, he tell Dub, the dumb-looking kid, to give him back his shotgun. He look mad and like he in a snit for being showed-up by the kid's shot.

"Where you boys headed?" Clyde say again. "And all dressed up and all," he say as he look at my suit.

"We taking Mr. Brady and Mr. Lester to they's granddaddy's funeral in Austin," I say, and truth be knowed, I even surprise myself with my quick lie. "They so broke up with grief, and," I point to the whiskey bottle in Clyde's hand, "kinda drunk, too. So my friend and me got to drive them."

"Goddammit, Clyde. What the goddamn hell's all the shooting for?" And it's the guy what is in the car's backseat. He be an older version of Clyde, in looks, and probly in meanness, too.

"Oh, hell, Buck," Clyde say. "I din't aim to wake you up. Jist having a little fun. And a drank, too!" He showed the bottle to Buck. Now Buck and Bonnie both was over by Clyde and taking turns snorting the bottle. It was jist about empty.

"Y'all got any more?" Clyde ast me.

"No, sir," I lie like a possum. "That's all we got."

"Well, I thank we oughta take a look in your car," Clyde say.

Then the woman from they car's backseat begin to whine about having to pee and for they to git back in they car so she can find a bathroom.

"Okay, okay, goddamnit. I'm coming!"

And next thing I knowed they was all in that car and taking off down the road. Me, I discovered that I taken a pee, too, and all down my britches-leg. Brady was standing beside me, touching my arm.

"Goddamn, Tom. Them was Bonnie and Clyde." His eyes look like saucers and his mouth was like a guppy's mouth.

"Yeah. That be them." I say, and I spit on the ground. Then I walk over to the dog scattered in several parts. Lester, he by me now and he have a butcher knife in his hand. Without no words, he begin digging a hole in the ground up past the ditch bank, and while I begin collecting the body parts, Benny and Brady come over and they help, too.

"You had a life and you cared about it, too," I say after the dirt was smoothed over the hole. I think I hear either Lester or Brady say something like Amen.

It was a few days later on, when we was driving back to Louisiana, that we heared the news that the Barrow Gang had robbed a bank in Alma, Texas, and a Piggly Wiggly store in Fayetteville, Texas, and had killed a marshal.

"Good grief!" Lester say in his teenage-boy voice. "We was right by them towns when we met up with Bonnie and Clyde! How about that?"

Yes, we was. We talked about it most of the way back to New Iberia, and jist before we get there I tell the boys that from now on the business was over. No more runs, no more selling booze, no more making it—no more nothing. I expected a lot of arguing and whining, but truth to tell, they all seem kind of relieved that I was ending things like I was.

Funny thing about it all, though. When we pull up in my front yard in New Iberia, we was suddenly surrounded by cops. About a half-dozen cars drove up real quick and about twenty-five men in dress suits and cop clothes, and all with guns in they hands, tell us all to surrender cause they got the drop on us. That was the end of the Darko Gang even if we had already ended it ourownselfs, and all four of us old boys took a vacation to the state pen at Angola, courtesy of the law enforcement folks of Louisiana.

They's not much to tell about my stay at Angola—where I was for near-bout two year of a five-year sentence for bootlegging—except to say that wudn't only the end of the Darko Gang, but it was the end of my marriage, too. While I was put away, Sally sold our house and car and everything else and disappeared with the money. Baptiste Junior tried to keep up with where she was, but he wudn't able to. We never got a divorce or nothing. I jist never saw her all the time I was in prison. She never wrote, never answered when I wrote, never visited me, never a phone call, even.

In the pen I fell back into my earlier occupation of timber-cutting and such-like. In-between-times, I also worked on the prison farm, walking behind a pair of mules in a cotton field, in the springtime, and then in the fall of the year pulling a cotton sack down the rows. I sometimes seen Benny and Brady and Lester at different times in the prison yard or a work detail, but mostly I was kept by myself. It was like the State of Louisiana still had no clear idea of what kind of a person I was. Sometime I was put with niggers and sometime with white men, but most of the time I was kept in a place off by myownself.

I found I had something of a reputation as the leader of the Darko Gang and I used it when I had to, mainly to keep all the assholes away from me. And prison is full of them, you can take my word for it. So, partly because I was a Indian, in a state where they's not sposed to be no Indians, and partly because I was thought of as a tough guy, I was genly left by myownself. And that was fine and dandy by me.

That playing the tough guy role remind me of a thing that happen one time when the Thomas Darko Gang was going great guns. You remember, too, that I mention something about Pretty Boy Floyd, how he was a hell-raiser at the same time the Barrow Gang and the Darko Gang and them was riding high? Well, Pretty Boy Floyd was the absolute other side of the coin to pig shit like Clyde Barrow. Now I don't mean to make a big hero out of Pretty Boy Floyd—me, I never met the man myself, though I heared a lot about him—but he was a whole lot cut from a different bolt of cloth than Bonnie and Clyde was. I heared he was part Indian, but I don't think that's the reason he was different from them two grubworms. Ruther he was always one who stuck up for his own kind—the poor folks all around the country—and certainly not to kill them flat-out in cold blood like Bonnie and Clyde done. No, he never turned on his own kind. They say sometime he would stay all night at some poor folks' home, never say who he be, and them folks never impolite to jist flat-out ask who he be, and come morning, after he done eat his breakfast and took off down the road, the lady of the house find a ten-dollar bill tuck under his plate or coffee cup. He was straight-up with his own people. It was them blood-sucking banks that he was hell on.

Anyway, what I-mo tell now has jist a little bit to do with Charles Arthur Floyd, who I heared never cottoned to that nickname Pretty Boy Floyd none a-tall. I guess it's my Pretty Boy Floyd story, what you might say. It happened when me and the boys was making a run from Fort Smith, Arkansas, to Tulsa,

Oklahoma. We was driving along the highway when we seen this old rattletrap Model T parked by the ditch. A poor-looking, skinny white feller in overalls was standing by the car, looking down at one of the tires. It look like he had been trying to fix it. The tire was jacked up and had no rubber tread a-tall, jist the metal rim. The man's wife was also scarecrow-looking and they passel of kids, about a half-dozen towheads, it look to me like, was skinny as wet cats. I remember it was cold that day—a strong, wet, rainy wind out of the north—coldern than a banker's heart. "Have some trouble?" I ast him. He seem suspicious of me, probly more of my dapper gray suit and tie than my dark-complected face. I repeated my question. "Yes," he say, "we had a blowout and ain't got no spare."

"Where you headed for?" I ast him.

"California. Aim to find work."

"Well, you not gonna git far on that bare rim," I say.

"Ain't got no choice," he say. "We can't turn back now."

"Come on, Tom," Brady yelled at me. "We got to git to Tulsa."

"Hold your horses," I say. Then one of the kids in the car start to cough and carry on, and it sound pretty bad. The mother held the little boy in her arms and rock him while he cough and cry. She looked straight at me, then to Brady and Lester and Benny in our car, and you could tell she was thinking: What more now, dear Lord?

Real quick, I turn from the man and go back to my car. I taken the spare tire off the back and come back over. I taken off my coat and say to the man, "Can I?" and motion for his lug-wrench in his hand.

"What you gonna do, mister? I can't take your spare, and besides, I can't even pay you for it."

"Nobody ast you to pay for it." And I hurried and put the tire on.

"That's real nice of you, mister, but I can't take your spare like this."

"That's okay. You need it more than me." I say.

He starts thanking me, and the wife, too, and I jist wave they thanks off.

"Here," I say, and hand the man a ten-dollar bill. "Git you some food, git some things for your car, and git some medicine for your child there."

"Mister, I shore appreciate your help, and I'm forever obliged to you," the man say. "Might I ast your name—so I can maybe pay you back someday?"

I turned toward him as I was gitting in my car and say, "I am Thomas Darko of Sherrillton, Louisiana, and we all be the Darko Gang."

"I heared your name before, Mr. Darko, and just remember that I am Jethro Seagraves, and I am in your debt."

"May God bless you and Jesus keep you," the lady spoke up now. I waved to them and then we was on our way, too. Now, I'll admit that I was touched by them folks and they condition, but I be lying like a possum if I don't tell you, too, that I was putting on some airs. Trying to do the old Pretty Boy Floyd thing, I was. I heared them tales how Pretty Boy give people ten, twenty dollars for a kitchen-cooked breakfast of ham and eggs, and I guess I wanted to put on the dog some, too. And, you know, after about a year went by, one day I got a letter addressed to me care of

Sherrillton. It was from Jethro Seagraves and with it was two bills, a ten and a five. He thanked me again in the letter and say that he and his family was in Bakersfield, California, doing fine, and for me to consider myself welcome in they home was I to come out for a visit.

Oh, before I forgit it, let me mention some more about what become of our gang. All three of them, Benny and Brady and Lester, all got paroled before me, and from time to time over the years I would run into them. Benny, he taken up work in a gas station in Bunkie and later ended up owning it. Lester and Brady both got some of them mail-out papers what ordained them as preachers. Lester become a Baptist preacher, and Brady joined the Pentecostals—or maybe it was the other way around. I can't remember. But I heared that they come to disagree so much on church differences, so folks tell me, that more than thirty years later they won't even talk to each other. I guess it's true what they say: crime does not pay. Especially when it leads brothers to be enemies of each other.

But looking back on my time in Angola, I have to say the most important thing that happened to me during that time wudn't something that actually happened to me or even that happened in the prison. It was something that happened outside. Early in December of 1934 I got the news that Mama, Baptiste Junior, my sisters Martha and Marie and Camille, and Camille's little girl, Suzette, was all killed in a wreck. It wudn't till some years later that I got all the details about the wreck, but as close as I can make it out, it happen like this: Baptiste Junior was driving his Ford flatbed truck and they was all in it, on they way to the woods by the river to pick up pecans, when he stopped at a railroad crossing, waiting for a train to go by, when somehow some of the train's cars come loose and run off the track and slammed into them. Everybody in the truck was killed straight out, way I heared it. That was my entire immediate family—not counting Sally, who, since she never come around none while I was in the pen, or even let me know where she was, couldn't be counted as family no more. I was now all alone. Daddy and Grandpapa had died about near the same time in 1921 or 1922, I can't remember exactly which, and when all the other ones passed on, that was it, no more close kin. Sho, I had, and still do, a lot of cousins in the Tunica and Biloxi groups, but no more folks that I could call Ofo, except for a couple of Mama's relatives that had lived away from Ofo Town for so long that not many of us Sherrillton Ofos thought of them as Ofos anymore.

My older twin-sisters, Martha and Marie—I hated for them to go so. They never had a good break with life. Both kind of feeble-minded and also deaf and dumb, they was still valuable people to us, to me. Even though they was never able to speak they thoughts out-loud, they had good ways to let you know how they cared about you—like cooking up a breakfast without they be ast to do it, or sewing a rip in you shirt when it got tore, and a whole lot of other little and important things. They was sweet girls, who though they was women in years, they was still little girls to us. Camille, my youngest sister, had a little girl by a Cajun guy who left her with no support, but that never stopped her or her little girl, Suzette, in making good lives with Mama and everybody. And Baptiste Junior, who never had the time to get to marry any girl but who was liked by a lot of them, passed on without leaving no kids behind him. Him who really loved kids and who was worshipped by little Suzette. And Mama going like that—she was the heart and backbone and the arms and legs of our folks. When she went, I knowed that a lot of my own life spark went with her.

I had been in the joint for a little more than a year, with what I figgered to be four more years to go on my sentence, when the news of they dying come to me. After that, and for a long, long time, I never keep track of my days, not caring if it was December 10th, or January 5th, or whatever. I no longer keep a tally of my served days or a tally of days to go. I give that up. All I did was work—plow, hoe, saw, tote, fetch, and run—and I only noticed if it was a frosty morning or a rainy one or a sunshiny one. Sometime about a year later, I begin to notice again the smells of cotton gins out away from the pen, and the tang of turpentine-cooking from the sawmills, and oil smells from close-by refineries. And then, duck-quacking and geese-honking when they fly by overhead, and finally a plover call in the springtime, and I guess I kind of come alive again. I realized, too, about this time, that I had pretty well even stopped talking to people, unless I was talked to by them first, and always in English, and all the time I was thinking Ofo things in Ofo and aware that now I might never git to speak the language again since everybody but me was gone. But more hurtful than that was the flash I had that I would never get to hear it spoke out-loud by anybody other than myownself. Then it was that I felt like I was a lone cypress in a cleared-off bayou bottom.

It was that same year of 1934 that the law finally bring down Bonnie and Clyde, catching them on a highway in northern Louisiana and riddling they bodies with bullets, both of them, with rifles and shotguns. I never exactly rejoice none, hearing that them two life-hating poisons got all shot up like they done, but I never actually went into mourning, neither. That 1934 was also the

year that they got Pretty Boy, too, and a bunch of others—
Dillinger and Ma Barker and her boys and Baby Face Nelson. And
all my folks. And Sally running off. It was a year of death. The
Sun still shined, but I paid it no honor, I am sorry to say.

Then, about the time I was gitting used to life in the pen, they paroled me. Told me I had to go back to Sherrillton and live there
while my probation was on. So I done that. I went back and
found that a Tunica relative was living in Mama's house. He of-
fered to move out so I could live there, but I told him to stay put.
I got a tarpaulin tent and set up my home down on the bayou, jist
inside the Tunica lands. I borried some steel traps and a shotgun
from another cousin and I taken up a life of hunting, fishing, and
trapping, like what I had done all throughout my young years.

Even though I wudn't sposed to do any traveling away from
Sherrillton, I went down a few times to New Iberia and around,
looking for Sally. The Four-Leaf Clover was long gone, so was
mine and Sally's house. And all the people that I could find that
had knowed us both never had no clue where she had gone. One
Saturday, I even taken the bus to Bayou Cane, but her grandfolks
never knowed where she was neither. She wudn't keeping in
touch with them none at all.

Now, I never had even a poor man's pot to pee in when I
come out the pen and so I had to start all over. Except for the
borrying of the steel traps and shotgun off my cousin, I jist about
had nothing at all. It was late summer when I got home, so I
taken my time, going easy, putting out a few bottom-lines in the
bayou. What I never eat of the catfish and bass I catched, I sold to
three country stores close by for between four cent and a dime a
pound. Some years, alligator hunting was good and I make good

63

money on they hides, and the meat was always a welcome thing. But coons, possums, mushrats, skunks, minks—these was my main ones for meat and skins. Midafternoons I gathered Spanish moss, dried and cured it out, and sold it for two, three cent a pound for packing material. All this wudn't no Thomas Darko Gang stuff, but I got by. Especially when I come to understand that I was probly going to be alone—really alone—for all the rest of my life. Even when I visited some Tunica cousins' houses, I always knowed that I was a genu-wine Lonesome Polecat. Sometimes when I was out in my push-skiff on the bayou, and I spected nobody else was about, I would talk to myself in Ofo, and it would seem to me like I could hear answers come back to me in the limbs and leaves of the cypresses and live oaks.

Like I say, I was a poor man, but not jist cause I had no property. No, I was poor cause I no longer had a family. This is real poorness. It can't never git no worse than that.

Then I went through a spell where I guess you might say I suffered from sampling my own wares too much. Cause I had also started back to making whiskey again—not to sell, since the Prohibition was ended, but jist for my own use and for the skill I always had in knowing how to make it good. It's the truth, and I kind of hate to admit it, but for a time I guess I was a out-and-out drunk. It got so I ruther set around my tent with a tin cup in my hand and a jug at my elbow—though mostly I never even fooled with the cup, jist took it straight out of the jug. It seem like all I cared about was running my trotlines and setting out my traps— even before the shikepoke season started—and jist puttering around the bayou. I had bought a little outboard motor, so that taken a lot of the labor out of my boat traveling.

It was sometime after legal trapping season opened that I

heard from a Tunica cousin that a friend of his thought that Sally might be in New Orleans. I found out as much as I could about the rumor, then got all slicked up—almost like I done back that time in the old days—and I borried a car and went to New Orleans. She was at a place called The Rainbow House, though there was no sign on the outside calling it that name, that I found her. I walk into the parlor and they was several women setting there in dressing gowns, and Sally be one of them. She knowed me right off.

"Tommy!" she yelled. "Why, how are you?" And she quickly taken me into a side room without no introductions to the other ladies.

"Sally." I say. "Sally." And I never said much else. We was hugging and kissing, and next thing I knowed we was in bed, catching up on married folks' things. After a while, when we was resting, I ast her how she come to be here. She told me how she got cheated out all her money—the money she got from our house and car—by a shikepoke jasper that jist taken advantage of her and hang her out to dry. When I ast for more details, she said "Oh, it's jist too damn bothersome to even have to try to explain—you understand, don't you, Tommy? My, it's so good to see you again." And we fell back to love-making.

When I started talking about us starting all over again, how I could buy another house and car and such, I noticed she get kind of quiet. I talked on, especially when she nodded her head a time or two, then I said I'd better go get dressed and start right away to gitting her moved back home. While I was buttoning my shirt and reaching for my coat, Sally say, "Tommy, before you go. Leave two dollars on the dresser there."

Real-dumb me, I say, "Why you need two dollars? Don't they

feed you enough around here?" I was trying to make a joke, because even being some kind of dumb I was figgering out what she mean.

"Naw, Tom. You're sposed to leave two dollars. I'm a businesswoman now, and I don't do it for fun no more."

"I wudn't fun then?" I say.

"Oh, it was fun enough. But I gotta make a living."

I started to get mad, but I knowed if I yelled or carried on it would jist make things worse. I spent a few more minutes trying to talk to her, but then they was a knock on the door and a woman's voice called to Sally to come help take care of the business that was stacking up out there in the parlor.

I couldn't say no more. I jist kissed her and said I would come back. And I did, the very next day, but an old lady there told me that Sally had taken the day off and was gone out and, no, she didn't know where she had went to.

I went back to Sherrillton, figgering it was probly jist as well. What's done is done. When things is over, they over. And I say other things like that to myself. But it wudn't jist like that. I don't mean to say that Sally and me got together again, because we didn't, and I never saw her again. But it taken a long time for it to be over for me, to be a thing of the past. Fact is, for a long time after, I would still take trips down to New Orleans and look all around for her. Or at least I would call myself looking all around for her. Sho, I was looking for her, alright, but I was also looking into a lot of whiskey and beer bottles, too.

One night, though, this New Orleans stuff all come to a head. It was in summertime, in the early evening jist as the Sun sink behind the levee. I already had quite a load on, whiskey and rum mostly, thinking about Sally and genly feeling down. I guess I was lonely. I go into this little-bitty bar close to Jackson Square—seem to me like the name Headless Horseman Saloon come to mind now—and I set there on the bar stool putting one drank after another away, and I git into a conversation with a white guy who was also no slouch for putting them away, neither. I start talking—too much, way too much for me—to this guy about not having anybody around who I can speak my language to. I know now that he wudn't at all interested in me or what I say, but he ast what language I mean. I say I think I'm probly the only person left in the world who speaks the Ofo Indian language. He laughs out-loud and say in a drunk voice, "Oh, you're an Oboe Indian, huhnn?" And he go on, "You're the Last of the Mugwumps, huh? Last of the Kumquats? Hah hah hah!" I try to correct him, realizing while I start to stand up that I be lucky if I can find my butt with both hands, much less talk to him like I make sense. Then I jist stop, look at his drunk face and open mouth, and think that I'm like that, too. And I go on to think, to decide: No more. No more of this. And particularly, no more talking to people like this guy. It be better to be lonesome than be a fool. Then I leave that saloon and head on back home.

5

In Colorado a Sioux Man Said "Peta"

I wish I could say that my World War Two experiences all
started like it done with a lot of other guys at the time, with a
telegram that read: Congratulations! You Have Been Drafted! Or
some such like it does in some of them picture shows. But it all
happened in a total different way. Fact is, I volunteered. Fact is, I
could of probly got out of the whole thing cause of my age. And
fact is, I was fool enough to pick what I heared was the toughest
branch to serve in—the Marines. It was like I was trying to hurry
up my life.

As the 1930s run out and the '40s come in, I was still living
off the bayou—fish, hides, meat, moss, and whiskey. But after
that last New Orleans trip, I had kind of turn my back on the rot-
gut. Oh sho, I'd still take a drink every now and then, and still
keep the old copper coil in operation, but it didn't have no holt on
me like it done before. I was also relearning, by using what little
memory from my boyhood days I had left, about the plants in my
country. Learning the old medicines again. I also made me a medicine pouch to wear all the time around my neck, and even if I

ain't sposed to tell all the power things I put in it, I can mention two of them: a plover wing and a half a handful of good Louisiana gumbo dirt. The other things, I hope you understand, is sposed to stay secret and private.

Anyways, I was doing okay about the time the war got started. I could always git something to eat out the bayou and the swamp, always sell a fish or a hide if I needed something, like coffee—which I always dearly love—or flour or a pair of shoes or some shotgun shells and so forth. I had a little house now, built on the bayou bank, and a pickup, and my own traps and guns. And I wudn't a fool about shine no more. I also had a young kid who hang around me most of the time—a Tunica cousin name Robert Vachon—who was learning a lot about hunting and trapping from me, plus a bit about medicine plants and things. He never spoke no Tunica, only English, cause by the time he come along the Tunica speakers was jist about to go the way of the Ofo speakers. Robert was a good kid, helpful to me, respectful, comical as a puppy, and I like him a lot. About the time Pearl Harbor was attacked, he was jist fifteen. Every day he would tell about the war what he learn about by listening to his folks' radio. When it seem real bleak for the American side in the Pacific Ocean, when it seem like the Japs was gonna take over all of the countries and islands in Asia and in the ocean, Robert more and more talked about enlisting. But he was too young. His daddy, Bernard, begged me to try to talk Robert out of running away to enlist. I promised to help, and I done as much as I could. I told Robert time and time to be patient, the war was gonna last long enough for him to git old enough to join up to go fight in it. Jist hold your horses, I say. Your time will come.

Well, sir, in January of 1943 Robert turned seventeen, and he was bound and determined to go. He was now of a legal age to enlist, but he still had to have at least one parent's signature to do it. Bernard finally agreed to sign for him. Then, somehow or other, that damn Bernard made me promise to go down with Robert for his induction, and I guess in the spirit of the enlistment I got carried away, too, and there I be, enlisting in the United States Marine Corps at the ancient age of thirty-seven, actually almost thirty-eight, and the next thing you know, Robert and me is sent to Baton Rouge for our physicals.

We got to San Diego, California, the place where the boot camp was held, and after a day or so—after a complete whirlwind of demanding things we had to do and all the while hearing the yells of the drill instructors—we was on our way to becoming Marines. About a week in our training, Robert started to having some pains in his chest. They x-rayed him and found he had an enlarged heart, which hadn't got found back in the physical in Baton Rouge, and the next thing you know Robert was give a medical discharge and sent back home to Louisiana. Poor Robert, he never made it to the war, and he died before he reach the age of thirty. But now here I was, stuck out there in the United States Marine Corps in San Diego, California, in a platoon of sixty men, and all back in my lonesomeness again.

I knowed right away that I don't care all that much for the Marine Corps, but I decide to think of it as jist like another time in prison—jist keep my mouth shut, keep my head down, do my work, and stay out of the way of assholes—overall, it wudn't bad, and I did learn a lot. The two DI's knowed right away I was a Indian, but except for calling me chief all the time, they never bothered me no more out of the ordinary than they did the other guys in the platoon. I was always real skinny-like, with no more meat on my bones than a grinnel, and my height, around 5 foot 6 inches, wudn't nothing to brag about neither, but I was in pretty good shape. For a thirty-eight-year-old man, I done pretty good keeping up with the teenagers.

One thing about the platoon I find out right away when I run into all kinds of different fellers—that all I-talians or Irish guys or Polacks is not out to kill you, like them I had run into before, that time in Chicago. Actually, I find that some of them guys was pretty decent people. Now, also, for the first time I was surrounded all day and all night by white people, and I had to learn they's all different kinds of people, and I don't jist mean Nation. I seen moody guys, happy-go-lucky guys, lost kid kind of guys, and some real bastards, too. I was the only Indian in the platoon, but they was two Mexican guys—which I think of as a different kind of Indian— one was a real nice guy, and the other one was a thief and liar and cheat. Like I say, I learn about different kind of people.

I was also surprised to see that most of the white guys was friendly to me, like they knowed we was all in the same big commode watching a big hand play around with the flush handle while we trying our best to keep our necks above the water level. I mean, for the first time in my life I was treated like a equal. It was something like the respect I got out of all them guys that used to hang around The Four-Leaf Clover, which I out-and-out earned by my actions, but this was still different. I had done nothing to earn they respect first, it was like they respect me, and everybody else there, jist cause we there.

They was one guy, though, name Briley that never seem to cotton to me. First, he would do jack-ass things like spit on the ground when I walk by and sort of mutter to hisself. I decided to ignore him. That wudn't easy to do since we not only had to go through boot camp together, we also got sent to the same squad of the same infantry company in the Second Marine Regiment. We finally had a scuffle one time, and when he see I would fight back, he sort of ease up on me some, but it seem he never really taken to me. We jist learned to walk easy around each other, like high-back tomcats up on they toes.

After I got in the Second Marines we begin infantry training in the hills of Southern California. We did the same thing later on in New Zealand. We hiked all over that goddamn green island, run dozens of field problems, and spent all the summer and most of the fall training, training, training.

One time when we was on one of our last hikes, going up one damn New Zealand hill after another, a big monsoon rain hit us real sudden-like. The winds was blowing hurricane-style— something I knowed about from Louisiana—but the sergeants and the officers kept yelling at us to keep walking, that none of us could turn back and that we couldn't hardly stay put neither. Only eight more miles, they say, pick 'em up and put 'em down, keep going and we git there soon enough. They was no jeeps or trucks to carry stragglers, so everybody jist had to buckle down and keep hiking. Pretty soon, jist as the wind and rain pick up even harder, stuff was blowing around in the air—helmets, radio set covers, even loose rifles—as guys had trouble holding on to all they equipment. It was pure-D dangerous.

Then a rifle come flipping by me in the air and hit Sergeant Mallory, our squad leader, right smack in the forehead. He was knocked out, with a lot of blood splattered all over his face. A corpsman hurried up to help him, while me and Briley was trying to git him to set up and come to. The corpsman told us that he had a concussion and that we had to fix it so he could be toted along.

73

"He's out cold. There's no jeeps or ambulances or any other wheels, so he's got to be carried. If he's left here in the heavy rain, even for a few minutes, he might drown. He's gotta be carried."

Me and Briley taken our rifles, looped a poncho between them to make a stretcher, and then we put Sergeant Mallory on it. We covered his face with another poncho, but such-like where he could breathe and still not suck up too much rainwater. Well, for the next eight miles, we toted that stretcher, ever once in a while taking turns with each other on the front end and the back end. When we finally got to the camp, I thought my arms was gonna fall off, they was so tired. Same with Briley. The lieutenant come over, thanked us for helping Mallory, and he give us light duty for the next couple of days. Sergeant Mallory, he got light-duty, too, and a few days later we was all back to usual.

The next morning after the hike was over and while the squad was off digging new slit trenches, I set outside our tent after chow. The Sun was out and I was honoring it, even though I wudn't giving no kind of impression I was. Briley come up and set down next to me. I didn't say nothing, and for a long time he didn't neither. Then he spoke.

"Darko, for an Indian guy, you're not bad."

"Thanks, Briley," I said. "You're not bad, either." Then I ast, "I take it you don't like Indians?"

"Yeah, that's right. But you're okay."

"And I say thanks again. Do you mind me asting what you got against Indians?"

"It's not just you. It's—you have to know about where I come from."

74

"Where's that?"

"Montana. Up there the goddamned Indians get everything given to 'em on a silver platter—education, health, land, water."

"Well, I don't know anything about Montana, but I know where I come from we don't get anything from the government."

By this time, I knowed a little bit about Indians in the West, reservations, treaties, BIA, and so on, but I had a hell of a time understanding Briley's resentment of them people cause of them things. We never solved the problems of white ranchers and Indians in Montana, and I think he still hated me for what I stand for—at least to him—but after that he never spit at my feet when I walk by. And he always nodded to me when we passed each other. I always nodded back.

Then in early November we boarded ships and left New Zealand. For many days we had no notion about where we was going. Rumors talked about us retaking the Philippines, or retaking Wake Island, or even that we was gonna be the first wave of troops to hit the coast of Japan. After all these years I am still surprised at my surprise back then when we finally learned that we had done grabbed the joker out of the card deck by the name of a place call Tarawa.

Tarawa. I had never heared of it. Even when they told us it was in the Gilbert Islands in the smack-dab middle of the Pacific Ocean, I still didn't know nothing about it. So, for about a week after we had this new name in our minds, our troopship, the *J. Abraham Scott,* chugged along in company with a whole fleet of ships—landing crafts, destroyers, cruisers, and them real beauties of the high seas, the battleships, what was all named after states of the United States. Hundreds and hundreds of ships, and thousands of men—but I bet a brand-new two-dollar bill I was the only Ofo there—and we was heading for this Tarawa.

Then one morning we waked up in our bunks to the sound of naval bombardment. Scattered at first, and then in heavy barrages—it run like that in waves—and continued that way for three days. A swabby told us that the gunfire was "softening up" the island for us Marines what was gonna be charging up the beach. I figgered with all that bombardment that they'd probly not be a live Jap nowhere on the island. I think all the other guys thought the same thing.

Finally, we git the order to stand by to board landing craft, and then it started for me. Outside, on the ocean, seeing all the smoky sky and hearing the naval gunfire, I was gitting my first taste of war. Quite a bit different from two hundred year ago when maybe five Ofos with bows and arrows face off against five or so Chickasaws and have at each other until one guy git hurt and everybody turn around and go home.

In the landing craft we was told the mouth of the lagoon on the main island, call Betio, was blocked up by Jap mines and barriers so bad that we was gonna have to wade in to the beach from way out. But don't worry, a swabby coxswain told us, most of the Japs done already been killed off in the naval bombardment.

Then I was in the water and it was up to my shoulders. I had to hold my rifle over my head. I felt a panic feeling, especially when water sloshed my face. The air around was filled with smoke and the noise of artillery guns from the ships behind us as they pounded that beach way off in the distance ahead of us.

I looked back one time and seen men behind me, they rifles held up over they heads like mine was, and behind them in the smoky haze of the ocean sky gray LSTs and destroyers and cruisers and Old Mary—the U.S.S. *Maryland*—and other battleships that I couldn't name. In front of me was about fifty or sixty Marines, and all of us wading now in chest-high water, rifles up high, and then the faraway rattle that at first I can't pinpoint, but then when I seen some water chopping up I realize is machine-gun fire. The Japs was shooting at us, and here we was expected to wade into the beachhead, and goodness me, we was still a good mile out! I-mo tell you, I figgered my time was up. Men in front of me and around me kept falling in the surf, and the churt-churt-churt of the machine-gun rounds smacking the water. Then I felt another panic feeling, more different from the first one, when I knowed I couldn't turn around and git back in the landing craft. And then I thought, "You never expected to live forever, did you?" And then I felt some better. I kind of speeded up my wad-ing in water, now about waist high, and I thought of a Ofo song about Sun Father and begin to sing it. Letting go my rifle with one hand, I reached down and touched my medicine bag under my camouflage shirt. My eyes was kind of blinded by the seawater and not too good-focused on that tiny island on ahead of me, all covered with smoke and blasted palm trees. Then everything went black.

I come to with the noise of shooting and explosions still going on all around me, but then I seen I was laying on the sand while Briley and a corpsman was busy wrapping my head in a bunch of gauze bandages. Talk about ache—whoo-eee, my head was hurting.

Briley grinned at me and I notice he was all bloody on his chest and neck. Then the corpsman stabbed my arm with a nee-dle and pretty soon I fell back into the black again. When I come to again, I was laying upside a concrete bunker wall with a bunch of other guys, ten foot or so up from the lagoon. I looked around, my head still hurting like hell, and seen that everybody around me was wounded in some kind of way, and then I remembered my head. I reached up and felt the big bandage covering all of the top of my head like a six-layered scarf. The racket of machine-gun fire and naval bombardment was still going on, and it feel like the whole island would shake when a twenty-pounder naval shell struck the beach. I felt myself gitting dizzy again, and then I looked at Briley again. He was looking at me, his light-blue eyes wide-open and wild-looking, and his mouth was moving. He was talking to me, but they was no sound coming out of his mouth. And then I noticed the bandaging around his throat and upper chest. "What? What you say?" I say to him, but he jist keep looking at me and then he died, his mouth and eyes still wide-open. I thought a thought for Briley then, but couldn't say it cause my throat is dry as sandpaper: "He had a good life and he cared for it." And so done all of them others laying all around me, and me, too. I cared about my life, too. While I was still staring at Briley I begin to notice the smell all around. I looked around and out at the lagoon. They was dead men by the hundreds laying in the water, bobbing up and down slow-like, like dark green corks and all bloated up to about it look like twice they normal size, and they was scattered all over the beach, too, all the way up to where the medical area was—where I was laying. All these years later I can still remember that smell and I can see without closing my eyes all them dead bodies bobbing up and down in the water and laying every whichaway on the sand.

Then I begin to notice the sand crabs. They was crawling on some of the men around me, and the more I watched the more I saw, until they was hundreds of them. Some of them was starting to eat on the dead men, and then I seen a couple of them even crawling up my legs. But seeing all them crabs never really bothered me none since I knowed they was only doing what they was sposed to do—clean they beach sand, eat, and jist live. Even when one bit down on my hand I don't worry none about it. I was already dopey and since I figgered I was gonna die anyway, then it wudn't no big deal. The sand crabs was a brownish-green, but I seen one that was kind of bright red, like a elderberry leaf after frost time, and I wondered, while my head was starting to spin again, if it was aware of itself as different from all the other sand crabs, and did it talk a talk that none of the other sand crabs knowed? I was staring out at all the killing and waste until I went under the blackness again.

When I come to, it was much later—many hours later—and I was back on a ship. It wudn't the *J. Abraham Scott,* cause it was too clean. When I seen everybody was wearing white clothes, I knowed then I was on a hospital ship. My head was a lot better, but it was still in a heap of bandages. I could still hear gunfire real far off, though no more big naval gunfire shells, and sometime a *whump!* of a mortar shell. But it sounded like the battle was winding down.

Over the next few days I heared that our battalion of the Second Marines had counted over 65 percent casualties. The other battalions taken near-bout the same, and the Eighth Marines, who followed us into the lagoon at Betio, also taken many casualties. The main fight for Tarawa Atoll lasted two days, and I heared tell it was the bloodiest battle in the whole Pacific war. I also learned that out of the ten guys in my rifle squad, including Briley and Sergeant Mallory, the squad leader, I was the only one to come out alive. I also discovered that I had lost my medicine bag, which I used to keep hung on my dogtags chain. I spect one of the medics found it and th'owed it away.

Just a bit over a month later, I was in a naval hospital in Hawaii when the First Shirt of the battalion come to visit me. He was fired-up and cheerful as all-git-out. He good-well oughta be since he never taken part in the Tarawa assault. First sergeants— in all regards a battalion's chief clerk and paper pusher—had been too valuable to risk wading the goddamn Pacific Ocean and helping to take over a tiny gnat's-ass-sized island like the rest of us grunts. At first thought I didn't want to see him, but then I figgered that he wudn't to blame for missing out on the fun at Tarawa. Wudn't his fault, and besides, he was always a fair man to me, had treated me right, and give me breaks. So I listened when he talked.

"Good news, Private Darko," he say, fidgeting with all kinds of paperwork in his hands.

"I-mo be discharged?" I ast.

"No," he say, a little embarrassed, it look like. Then he went on, "They're starting a new program in the Corps that's specifically designed for American Indian boys." His enthusiasm seem to come back like a horse ready to run. He went on to tell me about the Code Talkers, how Indians from all over the Corps was being picked to be radio operators. The idea was that Indians could talk to each other on the radio, or use Morse Code, in they own language and that way the Japs won't never understand them. So far, the First Sergeant added, they had mostly all Navajos, but they also had a few Cherokees and Choctaws and Comanches. Mainly, though, it was gonna to be a Navajo thing. But they wanted all kinds of other Indians, too. While he talked, I thought of Mama and Daddy and Grandpapa and all them now all passed on, and I recalled again, like I done a whole lot of times before, that it was near ten year since I talked to anybody in Ofo. I wudn't positive, but I was real sure I was the only one left. Once again, the Lone-damn-Ranger. I ast the First Shirt, "Who would I talk to?" And while he looked at me real funny-like, I started in laughing like a alligator, and I didn't stop until my head begin hurting again.

My head wound bothered me enough for quite a while, especially where my eyesight was concerned, that pretty soon I got my discharge anyhow and never got to join no Code Talkers, much less see no more combat. It was a funny thing, and I have thought a lot of time about it over the years. I go to war to fight the Japs, and I go to battle and git shot, and I never even seen a single Jap. Later on, when I be traveling around in South Arkansas or in certain big cities, I would sometime meet a Jap person. They was always nice and polite and respectful, and so I never held no grudge against them for shooting me, and I come to like them as people.

I had been back around Sherrillton off and on for a few years working the oil fields again, hunting and trapping and fishing most of the time, and some time going out away from home to work—the rodeo clown job I had in West Texas and in New Mexico that I already mentioned, for example, and the wheat-crop-following-after that I done in Kansas and Nebraska and South Dakota and Saskatchewan. And always I was by my lonesome. I even tried to find Sally again in New Orleans and Baton Rouge and New Iberia, and even went to Bayou Cane a couple of times, but she had jist plumb up-and-disappeared. Nobody knowed a thing about her. The last place most people knowed her to be at, jist like me, was New Orleans, but there the trail run out. Both her grandfolks died right after the war, and she never come back home to they funerals. I know, cause I went to both of them. I figger some mean-assed bastard probly carved her up with his knife one night and dumped her in the river. It seem like, since the war was over, they was a lot of them kind of mean people around. It was about that time that I taken to carrying a .38 and a straight razor again when I went out in public.

Sometime I be working in a wheat field with a bunch of other folks, and I could swear I hear my mama's voice talking in Ofo, and I turn around and she won't be there. Or, I be walking down a street in Kansas City and I see a skinny young blackheaded kid and I start to yell out "Leland!" and then I see it ain't him. Sometime I be in a dancehall, with it seem like two hundred people milling around, maybe I even be talking to somebody, but I be all by myself, if you know what I mean. One time I was in Colorado, working in the tater fields, working right alongside a Sioux man and woman, and they was talking to each other in they Indian language, when all of a sudden I heared the man say "peta" a couple of times, and I watched him point to a smudge-fire a few foot away. Now, in Ofo our word for fire is "peti," and so I ast the gentleman—after begging his pardon for butting in—about it, and he say, yes, "peta" means fire in Sioux. We tried out a few other words, my Ofo ones and his Sioux ones, and found some other close matches. Years later, when I told this story to Dr. William Allerton Payne, he said he was grateful for me telling him cause he say that confirmed his scholarly claim that Ofo is a Siouan language. Said he knowed of it cause of books he read, but this way showed a fine example of the close connection between the languages.

But for me, hearing Basil War Eagle tell me that about "peta," helped me a little bit not to feel my usual goddamn lonesomeness too bad. And I become good friends with Basil and his wife Mary after that. Through them I met a lot of other Sioux and Ute and Cheyenne people while I was following the tater crops, and then later the wheatfields.

Fact is, it was Basil and Mary that got me in them Hollywood movies I was in. They had been extras in some Westerns a few years before but had to leave Hollywood to find other work. Yeah, I know all the stories about Joan Crawford and Clark Gable and Gary Cooper and all them being rich as thriving gold mines, but the average bit player, especially extras, and especially Indian extras, find the gold mines harder to locate in Hollywood. But I never knowed all this before I went out there. I only found out about it later on.

I rode out to California with Basil and Mary in the summer of 1948, and right away Basil and me got ourselves all decked out in big feather-full warbonnets and buckskin outfits and planted on horses. We was sposed to be Cheyennes, but go and tell it to a Cheyenne. I got to yell out "Eeeh-yip-yip-yip!" on camera, and that qualified me as a speaking actor and so I was given the screen name of Chief Buffalo Horse. Me, who never had anything to do with buffaloes or horses either one in my whole life. Anyways, we got paid okay for the few days' work we got, and then we hung around some to see if other jobs would turn up. One day, in the casting line, I ast a big, brown-headed, light-skinned Indian man standing in front of me something, and when he turn around I see it is Jim Thorpe. After Basil and me introduced ourselves and we all three commenced talking, Jim tell us he's getting fed up with movies.

"I hate this damn town," he say. "I wish I could go back to Oklahoma."

He talked like that some more, then give us some good tips on good, cheap restaurants and invited us to come have some dranks together if we run into one another again, but then added, "You better make it quick, about them dranks, I mean, cause I'm trying to get out of this place."

When Basil ast him something about sports, Jim talked some about when he used to play football and baseball and run track, and how he made all the Indian people proud cause of what he done. Nowadays, he say, about the only living he can make is falling off of horses when the white guys shoot at him. And, he go on, he was real tired of it.

No, Hollywood wudn't no town for Indians. They wanted Indians in all them scenes in them Westerns all dolled up in feathers and such and setting up on horses, but they didn't want us to do too much talking and git in the way of the white guy who was genly playing the main Indian in the show. Indian extras usually had a tough time money-ways, trying to hang on out there waiting between Indian shows. I had one more on-camera assignment, and it was a movie about jazz music in what was sposed to be New Orleans. I got to talk on camera, in English, but later on they taken out all my lines and put some New York white guy's voice in place of mine. Say he sounded more Louisiana-sounding than me. I didn't git no screen credit that time.

After a few weeks I left California, and the War Eagles, and headed on back to Louisiana. Oil was making something of a comeback there, and for a while I roustabouted again some. They had a natural-gas boom, and I worked some at that, too. I was also getting some veteran's disability pay by now, and when that started coming in regular, I quit straight-out wage work and went back to my house in what I still call Ofo Town, though nobody else done it, and back to my life on the bayou. I had remade my medicine bag jist after I got out of the Marines and, back in Ofo Town, I was sometime called on by Tunica kin to do some doctoring with plants and what-all. I figgered I was back there for good.

6

In the Name of Science

One day, while I was skinning some coons by my back door, I heared my two dogs bark in that way they got to let me know a stranger is coming. I ducked around to the front of the house to see who it be, and it was this old white man dressed in a brown suit and toting a brown leather briefcase. He was tall and thin, with a full head of white-gray hair and he had a slight stoop to him. We nodded to each other and then he say, real gentlemanly and in a voice that showed right away he wudn't no Louisiana man, "Do I have the honor of addressing Thomas Darko?"

"Yes," I say. "I am Thomas Darko."

"Mr. Darko, I am Dr. William Allerton Payne, of the Smithsonian Institution in Washington, D.C.," he said. Then he added, with a sad but friendly smile, "We had the honor of meeting one another many years ago, but I expect you probably don't recall it."

"No, sir," I say. "I can't say as I do." And it was true. I couldn't recall ever seeing this feller before, much less meet him.

"Well, I'm not surprised. You were a very small boy then. I was here visiting your parents and grandfather—please pardon the possible rudeness in my mentioning of them—I was visiting them, as I say, as well as meeting numerous Biloxi and Tunica folks along with your Ofo relatives."

"Well, yes, sir," I say. "That mus' all been a long time ago. All my folks, sir, have all passed on."

"Yes, I know, Mr. Darko. That is why I'm here. And, please, will you accept my condolences on their behalf?"

I nodded my head for his respect.

He went on to tell me that he was representing the Smithsonian in a new program they was setting up having to do with Indian languages. He say they was recording languages with tape recorders, making records and dictionaries and such, and that was why he come to see me.

"You are, by all accounts, Mr. Darko," he said, "the last speaker of the Ofo language."

Now I knowed nobody else around Sherrillton talked Ofo, not since Mama and them all got killed in that truck wreck, but I knowed in a vague way of some other relatives living away from Sherrillton who I thought still might talk it.

"Well, now, sir," I said, "they's my Aunt Gustine, over at Shreveport, and all her kids. What about them?"

"I'm sorry to say, sir," Dr. Payne said, "your Aunt Augustine passed away ten years ago and apparently none of her four children grew up learning any of the Ofo language at all." He paused and then added, "I'm sorry, sir. I perceive you had not heard of your aunt's death?"

"No, I never," I said. "I appreciate you telling me."

"I certainly didn't intend to be simply the harbinger of sad tidings," he said. "I hope I haven't offended you by my intrusiveness."

"No, sir," I said. "I am not at all offended, and I be thankful

88

for your words." Then I thought to add, "What about my cousin, Rejean LeGarde over in Longview, Texas? I knowed he used to know some Ofo, but not a lot."

Dr. Payne ducked his head slightly and coughed, then he say, "Again, I'm sorry to say, Mr. LeGarde passed on about five years ago."

I set there a minute, thinking.

"Then I am all alone."

"Yes, it would appear so, sir. You are the last of the Ofos."

Then he begged my pardon and ast to be excused while he went back to his car, he say, to git something he forgit to bring with him. Instead, I think he jist want to give me some time to myself. Cause when he come back in about five minutes, I never seen anything he bring back with him, and he left that brown leather briefcase on my front door step. Anyhow, I appreciated his thoughtfulness, and while he was gone I thought about all of them now gone—Mama, Papa, Rejean, Aunt Gustine, Grandpapa Arceneaux, and all my brothers and sisters—and I spect I felt more than ever before like a lonesome pine tree. But when Dr. Payne come back, I remember my manners and I invite him in for some coffee or ice tea. He say thanks much, he would like some ice tea, say he too old to drank coffee in the late part of the day, but he say he love ice tea. Me, too. Especially since I give up whiskey-drinking some time back, why, ice tea, with a lot of sugar in it, made up for it, I spect.

I got him to stay to supper. I put some fresh coon meat in a stew I had slow-cooking on my kitchen stove, made a pan of corn-bread, and we had more ice tea. In the meantime, Dr. Payne told me about the purpose of his visit. Seem like he wanted me to come to Washington, D.C., for a while to help preserve the Ofo language on records and help them make a dictionary. I give it some thought, liked the idea of traveling again, but I wondered about the good of saving a language on records and in a dictionary when they wudn't nobody but me left to talk it. He say that In the Name of Science was the reason, almost like he was talking about a church or something. He say I would git paid good, have my hotel paid for, too, and would be contributing to Science. He say for me to mull it over and let him know in the morning. I invited him to stay the night, but he say he already have a hotel room in Alexandria and would come back in the morning. But before he left, he showed me a book he dug out of that brown leather briefcase, and in it they was a picture of my Mama and Papa and all of us younguns, and they was Grandpapa Arceneaux, too. Dr. Payne told me how he taken that picture when he visit in 1909, when he first come to our country as a young scholar of our ways. Now, I never had no pictures of any of my family at all, and seeing them all like this was a little too much for me. They was Papa, wearing a white shirt all buttoned up to the neck and wearing his little-bitty black dribbly moustache, and Mama, a lot taller than him, wearing a white blouse with long sleeves and all buttoned up to the neck, too, and her hair in a bun, Grandpapa in dark overalls and a ragged suit coat, my spindly brothers Leland and Andrew and Baptiste Junior, and my twin sisters Martha and Marie. Dr. Payne pointed out the two littlest kids in the picture, and they was me and my little sister Camille. In the picture I was a scrawny little duck-egg-looking thang, all eyes and a bowl-over-the-head haircut and dark-skinned as a dirt-dauber, and Camille was a fat little two-year-old holding onto a cornshuck doll. Before he left to go back to his hotel room, Dr. Payne give me the book with the picture in it, told me it was mine to keep, and that night

I read some of it. It was about little groups of Indian people in places like Louisiana and Arkansas and Texas—where they wudn't sposed to be no Indian people left. They was even a picture of John Desriusseaux—or Old Man Jack Darrysaw, as people call him—and one of Jed Thompson, two of the Quapaw people I meet years ago in Arkansas. Sesostre Youchicant, a long-time Tunica chief, was there, too, and Chief Volcine Chiki and Chief Eli Barbry, what was also Chiefs of the Tunicas, too. I already knowed what I would tell Dr. Payne in the morning.

We left for Washington, D.C., two days later. It taken me a day to fix it so Ignace and Louise Paul, a Tunica cousin of mine and his wife, could come live in my house while I be away. Of course, they jumped at the chance, since they was living with Louise's folks, and was glad to git by theyselves for a time. That time I went out to Hollywood to be in them picture shows they stayed in my house and kept things together, so I knowed they was dependable. Me and Dr. Payne drove in his Oldsmobile to D.C. We taken two days to do it, with him letting me share with the driving. During the trip I got to know him better and even though I liked him since that first day at my house, now I could say that I really liked him. He was, in all respects, a real gentleman. He had some of that old Indian way about him, probly cause he had spent so much time with Indian old-timers who practice respect on a daily basis.

On our trip north, Dr. Payne and me talked over a lot of things. He told me about Indians all around the country, and how it was now, in the 1960s, things was beginning to look a little better. Education and health and housing and such was improving. He say he was extremely pleased—his own words—that my neighbors and close relatives, the Tunicas and Biloxis, was reorganizing as a formal tribal group and looking at going for state and federal recognition. And he even explained, in the best way I ever knowed of, what that idea of recognition mean. It had never been clear to me before.

He also told me that at the Smithsonian I would be working directly with Dr. Matthew B. Smight, who was becoming known as the main authority on my tribe and language and other Indian tribes in Louisiana. He tell me he come to Louisiana to see me, instead of Dr. Smight, cause he wanted to see my home country one more time before he passed on to the Great Beyond. Even though, he say, Dr. Smight could use the fieldwork, whatever that mean. I was disappointed that I wudn't going to be working with Dr. Payne, but he say he retired now, and he left the day-to-day work to Dr. Smight and others. He say he still come around on occasion, so it wudn't going to be like I never git to see him. He laughed a little, then said, "I imagine Dr. Smight is going to have quite a bit of serious scholarly readjustment ahead of him, now that you're joining our staff."

I ast him what did he mean, and he tell me that Dr. Smight had published a long paper in a high-tone journal of Indian kind of scholarship, in which he says Ofo is entirely a dead language and that the tribe no longer exist. Said he tried to urge Dr. Smight not to be too quick to put his work out there in a paper until he checked all "avenues of possibility"—which I guess means me— but that the young scholar was in a big hurry to publish his work. Now that I am here, Dr. Payne say, Dr. Smight was going to have to "modify his contentions," or in other words, he done got catched with his britches down.

I stayed at Dr. Payne's home for a few days after we got to

Washington until the Institution give me a special advance on my salary so I could rent my own place. I found a rooming house jist a few blocks from the Institution, which was also a great-big museum and all, and a whole lot of offices. Dr. Payne and his housekeeper, a colored woman name Selma, showed me some of the places in Washington—the White House, the Senate building, the Washington Monument, Arlington Cemetery, and good little grocery stores and such. Oh, and by this time I done learn that colored or black people don't like the word "nigger," what I been using all my life. I never meant no disrespect at all. I jist don't know no better till I am told by Dr. Payne. Coloreds or black people or Afro-Americans is the names I learn to use after I come to Washington in 1963. Negro, though, was the main word to use.

Then, on the first Monday after we git to D.C., Dr. Payne taken me to the Smithsonian, where I was to work. Right away I meet Dr. Smight, a big, tall, heavy-set blond-headed young man, less than thirty, who I can't help but notice don't care a bean-hull for me. Jist the way he introduces hisself: "Thomas," he say, sticking out his hand to shake mine, "I'm Dr. Smight. We're pleased to have you with us." And while his mouth is grinning to beat the band, his eyes are mean and sharp-like, like little knifes. He remind me of Frankie McErlane that I run into that time long ago in Chicago, and I knowed right away to be on my guard with this guy. But I'm used to guys like him, so I come back with, "Matthew, it's real pleasant to make your acquaintance, too," and oh, he don't like it when I give him back that first-name stuff.

And then I meet Dr. Bledsoe and Dr. Overstreet, two other young anthropologists specializing in Indian people in the American South. Bledsoe, he is a expert on music and art, and Overstreet is one on Virginia Indian languages. I also meet a Canadian

Indian guy, about my age, name Wilson Bill. He say he is from the Kaska Tribe in British Columbia. I start to tell him about going through British Columbia that time I taken the job on the Alcan Highway up in the Yukon, but he don't seem interested. He jist walk away while I'm talking to him. Fact is, I hate to say it, but this guy Wilson Bill is the snottiest Indian person I ever did meet. After that, in all the time he was there until he quit and when back home to Canada, Wilson Bill would jist barely say hello to people, and then he act like he doing you a big favor at it. So, after that, ever time I see him, I say, jist as polite as I can, "Good morning" or "Hello" or whatever, without no worrying none whether he answer me.

It never took long for Dr. Smight to show his colors. Ever time I bring up something about Ofo language or other things at home, he want to argue. Me, I never argue. I jist present my information or my statement and let him rattle on. I begin to make long lists of Ofo words, in ABC order and give the English equals for him off to the side of the paper. In jist a couple of weeks, my list was more than four times longer than the old one they had in they museum records. Smight don't like that, and he want to have a goddamn debating society over each one of them words. When he start doing that, I jist give the old Indian fish-eye look and they ain't nothing he can do but drop the subject.

But he would go out of his way time and time to let me know he was a *PH.D.,* with capital letters, or *DR. SMIGHT,* again in capital letters, and that I was jist a ignorant coon-ass Indian who might not even be a real Ofo, was the way he hint a lot of the time. Always letting me know my place. Take for an example the time him and Dr. Bledsoe was showing me some old Ofo and Tunica things—buckskin clothes, bear robes, pottery, baskets,

94

carved things. Smight took a long flute made out of a switch-cane out of its glass case, and as he is telling me how it's an Ofo flute, I can remember my grandpapa playing one jist like it, maybe even the same exact one. While Smight is talking about it, holding it up in his hands, I reach for it, and he pull it away from me, with a frown on his face, saying such shit like, "I'm sorry, Thomas. I'm afraid only qualified specialists are allowed to handle such valuable artifacts. You can certainly understand, can't you?" I jist barely can say yes and after that I block out everything that shikepoke be saying.

With Dr. Bledsoe it was a whole different situation. He never ast me rude, too direct questions, and he never acted like I was a five-year-old. Instead, he treat me like a normal young thirty-or-so man—same age, too, he was, as Smight—usually treat a man who is nearly thirty year older than him. Me and him done some recording of me speaking Ofo—something I had done decided I wudn't going to do with Smight—mainly, cause as a musicologist Dr. Bledsoe knowed all about taping and such. I always enjoyed that work.

But I also had a social life outside the Institution. Right away, I met a black woman about my age name Melba, who was a cook and waitress in a little restaurant close by the rooming house I lived in. Pretty soon we was keeping company. Now, I had been around black people a lot back home, but never in a close personal relationship like this. Melba was a quiet, hardworking woman who loved to see people be happy, and I enjoyed her company very much. Her husband had died years ago, leave her with two kids to raise, which she done real good cause now they was married and Melba was grandmother to four or five little kids. She had never remarried. Before I come on the scene, she had been involved with a younger black man, a real wheeler-dealer name Shep. Shep was sort of a crook and a real tough guy, but when Melba found about his real nature and ornery ways, she got shet of him. But, Melba told me, Shep don't like that none, and she heared that he say he was going to git even with her.

Well, I taken to carrying my straight-razor again, and sometimes my .38. Me, almost nearly a old man—doing these young, tough guy things. I thought I was past all that stuff. One night I was walking up the three flight of stairs to Melba's place when all of a sudden Shep step out of some hallway shadows and push me back down the stairs. I fell about fifteen foot, rolling backwards down the stairs. I got knocked out and got a sprain arm and a bad bruise on my leg.

When the Smithsonian people heared about my close call, I was talked to by Dr. Smight and Dr. Overstreet about my "carelessness." Smight said I got to be more careful. "You are too valuable an artifact—uhh, a person—to be lost by such a stupid thing as a spurned boyfriend's jealous rages," is the way he put it. Both Smight and Overstreet kept going on about how my "demise" would be a blow to Science. Before they one-sided interview with me concluded, Smight tell me the Institution was taking a $75,000 life insurance policy out on me. When I seen the look in Smight's eyes when he say this, I started to worry in a whole different way. I knowed I'd be looking behind my back more and more now, jist to see if he wudn't standing there with a stick in his hand.

About a week later, I was walking back to my place from Melba's late at night when Shep and another guy stepped out of an alley and started shooting at me. Three or four pistol shots and a blast of buckshot—all the time I was running my butt off. I lost them after a couple of blocks and was able to hide in a tailor shop that was still open. I was scared as hell. It was like Tarawa all over again. Real slow, I looked all over myself to see how many times I been hit. The answer was—a whole lot. But not me, only my clothes. They was three bullet holes in my coat and britches, and the whole tail of my coat was chewed up by the charge of buckshot. But my body, myownself, had not even been grazed.

Of course, Smight and Overstreet raised holy hell all over again, and Smight said he was going to double my insurance policy. I don't know if he ever did do it, and I don't really care. While they both ranted and raved about my Duty of Science and so on, I had a sure ace card in my watch pocket. And finally I sprung it. I told them that Shep and his pal had been arrested. A cop had seen them shoot at me. With a witness like that, I was told, they was going away for a long spell.

I was really gitting fed up with Smight. If it wudn't for Dr. Payne—who I visited jist about once a week—and Eric Bledsoe, I think I would of walked out of that job long before I finally done it. Dr. Payne's health was declining. I knowed he was old, but until recently, before he had some strokes, he was in real fine health for a man eighty years or so old. His mind was still sharp, maybe even more so, and he never complained about anything. So I kept on doing my word-listing and language-recording, and having my visits with Dr. Payne and my two-nights-a-week visits with Melba.

One day I seen a notice in the morning paper that a great-big Indian conference was going to take place in a Washington, D.C., hotel. It was an organization called the American Association of Indian People, or some such. I decided to go. It seem like of late I was spending less and less time with Indians, and I was looking

97

forward to the whole different kind of atmosphere that's found in a Indian get-together—with people more calm and accepting of each other, not squirming to out-do each other, jist be theyselves, and practicing they lives of daily and mutual respect.

I got down to the hotel about noon. The conference had jist got under way. In the main floor auditorium, the room was full of several hundred people, mostly Indian, and a speaker was jist being introduced. Then I turn around and almost bump into this young Indian guy, standing right by me. He was about twenty or so, on the skinny side, with black intense eyes looking out of a pair of black horn-rim glasses. His hair was on the longish side, near-bout to his shoulders, and he toted a battered old black brief-case with no handle on it and a couple of paperback books in one hand and a rolled-up towel with some clothes in it in the other one.

We both say excuse me at the same time and kind of back up together out of the crowd a bit. He kind of dressed like me—a light jacket, baggy pants, and no tie. And then I notice that him and me about the onliest ones there not wearing no tie. And to top that off, we ain't neither one of us got a name tag on like everybody else. "Big doings," he say. "I gotta have a cigarette," the kid say, and motion like for me to join him in the foyer outside the room where the speaker was holding forth on the podium in front of the big crowd. She was a heavy-set white lady draped in all kind of silver and turquoise jewelry and wearing a fancy deer-skin gown what was worth probly three or four little-bitty farms back in Louisiana. She was going on about "initiative" and "boot-straps" and "the welfare trap." She oughta git together with Overstreet. He was all the time complaining about Indians git every thing handed to them free. Now I ain't never been much to smoke, except to share when somebody invite me, like this kid was doing. He lit up one for me and for him, and we stood to-gether, with the lady's voice still carrying through the open door.

"My name is Simon," he say. "Pueblo from New Mexico."

I tell him my name and when I say I'm Ofo from Louisiana, he seem surprised. Say he heared about Ofos, said he had even stopped at Tunica the past week, but that he never knowed they was any of us Ofos left. We chatted about that a bit, and I ast him what the rich white lady was going on about.

"Oh, she ain't a white lady. She's a Mohawk from upstate New York. She works for the Bureau of Indian Affairs and is also a big wheel in the Republican Party."

"Indian, huh?" I say. "Well, I run into a lot of white-looking Indians in my time, but not too many look like they Madam Moneybags."

The kid laughed.

"Yeah, she is for sure well-heeled. They say her husband is a corporation president, with his hands in all kinds of money-making pies—like oil and timber and gas."

"You don't say," I say. "Well, then, if she is so well-to-do, why is she hanging out with Indian folks?"

The kid laughed again. I'm already sizing him up as a plenty-smart young feller.

"That's how she got so wealthy—she and her husband," he say. "His companies are wheeling and dealing on lands that until recently belonged to Indians."

"You mean through this termination that she talk about?" I ast, remembering something of her harangue about the need for Indian people to be "emancipated from Federal responsibility," or some such.

99

"Yes, that's how it goes," he said. "Tribes are terminated, the land is allotted to tribal members, who are then supposed to be like other private American citizens, and then they are often cheated out of it. At the same time, great parcels of it, particularly with forest lands, are being bought up by entities like the Great United Toilet Paper Company."

"Which Mr. Moneybags happens to be chairman of the board of," I say.

"You got it," the kid says.

"I don't know," I say. "I don't know much about all that. I jist wanted to come down and be around Indian people for a change." Simon ast what I do, and I tell him about the Smithsonian work. He said he was a student in a college in New Mexico and that he wanted to be a writer. When I ast him about how he go about trying to be a writer, he tell me that he had wrote maybe a dozen stories and maybe a hundred poems. I tell him they ain't no "going to" about it—he was already a writer. He stopped and thought for a moment, then he say, "You know, you're right. I am a writer."

They wudn't no chairs in the foyer area, so we both set down on the floor close to a ashtray. We told each other about our homes, our folks, what our tribes was like. I liked the kid a lot. He was smart, respectful, and full of a whole lot of hope for Indian people everywhere.

Then the session in the ballroom was over, and right away, while people started milling around in the foyer, greeting each other and lighting up cigarettes, Madam Moneybags and her group of folks come out and they stand right next to me and Simon. A young white guy in her crowd, with a expensive suit and tie on, come over and spoke to us. At first, I didn't understand him.

"Where are your badges?" he repeated.

"We don't have any," Simon said.

"You have to have a badge before you can take part in the conference," the guy said.

"How do we get them?"

"Well, you see that desk down there," he said, pointing. "That's the registration area. Just show them your tribal enrollment card, pay ten dollars, and you can come in."

"Do *you* have a tribal enrollment card?" Simon ast the guy.

"Uh, no," he say. "But I'm with the Bureau. . . . "

"Oh, the Bureau," Simon say. "And that makes all the difference in the world, doesn't it?"

The guy look like he been dashed in the face with a bucket of water.

Then Madam Moneybags barged over and in a loud voice said that if we don't have an enrollment card or ten dollars, then we got to leave. She had on a big name tag that say "Princess Silver Rainbow" and underneath another name, Beth Lilliworth. They is also a gaudy Goldwater for President button on her lapel. I look around, and a couple of Indian people who are watching what's going on seem to be embarrassed cause of the woman and her little white guy lapdog.

Suddenly I say, "I don't have no enrollment card."

"What?" Princess Silver Rainbow said. "How can you expect to come around Indian people if you don't have a card."

"I've been Indian all my life and I have never had a card." I say. Several people is watching us. The Princess don't like this.

"You can't be Indian unless you got a card," she said, her voice louder now.

"I've got a card, but I don't have ten dollars that I want to spend just to be around other Indians," Simon say. "Why do you need our ten dollars?"

Princess Silver Rainbow jist glared at him, and then at me.

Simon took hold of my arm and real gently-like got me to go with him to the front door.

"To hell with this," he said. "Let's go."

We go out the door, and then stand and breathe the air.

"It will be different one of these days," he say. "There's gonna be a real awakening in Indian Country one of these days, and you know, I have a feeling that Princess Moneybags and all her kind will make their choices. They'll go with all the rich white folks. Along with all the BIA poodle types. And then Indian people will be left alone. It's gonna come. We just have to wait."

I nod, cause I like the kid's spirit even though I don't know much about what he's talking about.

Then he go on.

"I've been traveling around a whole lot this past year—mostly in the South. Like at Tunica last week, you know?" I nod. "I was in Texas and Arkansas and Louisiana and Alabama, Georgia, Florida—all places where there's not supposed to be any, or at least a very few, Indian people. But, you know, I find Indians all around—Indians are everywhere."

I agree with him and say that has been my experience, too.

"Well," I say. "I better git back to my place. Workday tomorrow."

"I know where there's gonna be a party—an Indian party," the kid say. "You want to come? There'll be a lot of folks from out my way—New Mexico and Arizona."

I think for a minute, but I'm feeling tired. I say, "No thanks, but thanks for the invite."

"Be good, older brother," Simon say to me, and we shake hands.

"You, too, little brother," I say.

"Look me up in New Mexico sometime."

"I will. Look me up in Louisiana."

And I watch him walk a block or so before I turn and start my walk back to my rooming house.

Then one day Dr. Smight and Dr. Overstreet and Dr. Bledsoe taken me out to the Pamunkey Reservation, "to see some Indians," they said. They say they want to show me they Indians in Virginia, jist a tomcat-flinging distance from D.C. So we start out from Washington real early in the morning, a frosty cold day in February. We drove through the Virginia countryside to Pamunkey, a good two-hour trip in Overstreet's Cadillac. I'd been in D.C. for about five or six months and hadn't seen much of the countryside around, either in Virginia or Maryland, although in D.C. I'd started spending a lot of time in late afternoons and on weekends in several of the parks along the creek a mile or so from the Institution offices. So the Virginia trip was real welcome to me. The cold fog hovering over the winter fields and on the edges of fencerows, the many creeks and rivers we cross over, remind me of back home in Louisiana.

We got to Pamunkey about eight, stopped at a roadside cafe jist outside of town and had breakfast, then we drive on out to the reservation. We met first with the agent there, a man name Gaines, and then went on to the community center. Several Indian ladies wearing Mother Hubbard bonnets and heavy cotton work dresses was set up at a long table selling baskets and canned vegetables. I watched them watching us coming up to they table, with they "greet-the-white-folks" looks on—very grave, watchful, and totally respectful—and then they seen me. They still showed the graveness and watchfulness, but they had smiles in they eyes when they greeted me. Nobody introduced us, but I was used to that. I returned they graveness and watchfulness, too, I guess, and I made sure that they could see my own Indian way of smiling with my eyes. I bought a jar of chow-chow.

Next we was taken down to a schoolhouse. It was a one-room, a building made out of unpainted lumber. They was desks with a metal runner connecting them all together, all in lines like little choo-choo trains. They was probly about fifteen pupils, and all was Indian kids of all kinds of shades of dark and light skin, with the boys wearing faded blue overalls and the girls wearing light-colored cotton dresses with full sleeves all the way down to they wrists. They teacher, a middle-aged white man wearing a black suit, was standing in front of the class reading to them out of a book. They was a great-big American flag nailed to one wall in the back of the class, a blackboard on the wall behind the teacher, and several windows on both the sidewalls. A potbellied wood stove, putting out a little bit of heat, was in the center of the four rows of desks. The agent Gaines give our names to the teacher, who I heared be called Gant or Grant, and told that we come from the Smithsonian on a fact-finding tour. The teacher welcomed us, hustled a couple of kids out of they desks in the far-side row and invited us to sit down in they empty spots. Over-street and Smight, who was kind of overly heavy-set, had a hard time scrunching into them little seats, but me, still scrawny as a banty, slid right in with room to spare. Bledsoe, tall and skinny, didn't have much trouble scrunching into his seat neither, though his long legs had to spider out in the aisle for extra room. Behind us, at the back of one of the middle rows, two of the bigger boys was whispering to each other, and they was using Indian words. Pamunkey, I spect.

It looked like the kids was all between the ages of six and sixteen and I guess in different grades. The littlest ones set together at the head, the middlest ones in the middle, and the biggest ones in the back, so I guess they was grouped into grades. But I couldn't swear to it since nobody told us what the grade set-up was. We was setting there, observing Gant or Grant while he read something about a poem lovely like a tree. The two bigger boys was still whispering to each other. All of a sudden, the teacher slammed on the brakes with his reading and yelled out at them, "Wesley" and "David," and he hustled back where they was.

"Were you speaking Pamunkey, Wesley?" the teacher demanded. But before the boy could answer, which I doubt he would of done anyhow, the teacher turned and demanded the same thing to the boy called David. The boys, now jerked up on they feet, stood looking down at the floor.

"You know the rules here, you two." Gant or Grant said. "Only English is to be spoken in this classroom. Now you make it necessary for me to make an example out of you for our visitors, particularly to show them we're not at all lax in our educational duties here at Pamunkey Day School."

The boys was still quiet, jist standing there looking down at they feet.

"Cynthia," the teacher called out. "Bring the strap." And one of the bigger girls got up from her seat and got a leather strap from behind the teacher's desk, the kind use to be used for honing straight razors, and bring it to him. The girl never looked at the teacher or none of us while she was fetching that strap. I looked over at Smight and Overstreet and they was jist setting there with slight smiles on they faces. Dr. Bledsoe, though, had a frown on his face and was jist looking out the window, like he didn't want his mind to even be on what was going on in the room. While the teacher was making the boys bend over they desks, Dr. Bledsoe said, "Mr. Gant, would you prefer that we excuse ourselves, if you're going to administer disciplinary measures?" Dr. Bledsoe said.

"Oh, no, sir. That's not at all necessary." Mr. Gant said, smiling. "Indeed, it behooves me to urge you remain as you are, in order to witness the efficacy of chastisement in order to forestall the practice of bad habits."

And then I was remembering way back, many years ago, when Old Lady Mitchell would whup me or Camille or Rejean for slipping up and saying a Ofo word, and the same thing for Tunica kids when they done it in they language. Always, she say, it was for our betterment. I remembered, too, way back in the time of the 1927 Flood, a real-big event in our part of the country. It was what's known as a Great Flood, and not jist the time of a regular flood. It had rained steady for much of the winter of 1926 and into the spring of 1927, and the water rose and rose. Hundreds of people in Louisiana and Mississippi and Arkansas was drowned, many thousands of livestock lost, and thousands of acres of crops lost, and even before it actually happened everybody had knowed for a long time that it was going to happen, that it was going to be a Great Flood. I hurried on home from New Iberia to help out my folks. By the time the water finally come in on us, we was safe— all of our family and a bunch of others—was on top of one of the several burial mounds that are now part of the state park close to

Sherrillton. For hundreds of years our folks have always gone to
these mounds, and others like them, during highwater time, and
this time wudn't no different for us. Anyway, we was there, in
tents made out of canvas scraps and tree bark, when some park
rangers come by in a motorboat and demanded we vacate the
mounds before we ruint them. We refused to move. One guy got
so mad at us that he say if we didn't move he'd start shooting
everybody, until finally another ranger, a older man, told him to
leave us alone. And he said a interesting thing, something I genly
don't expect to hear from a shikepoke: "Let 'em alone, Bob. I
think they know what they doing. And I think they will still be
doing it many, many hundreds of years from now, too. We need
to learn when to back off and leave these people alone."

Oh, I wish I could of told this Gant to leave them kids alone,
but I never. And Overstreet or Bledsoe or Smight didn't neither. It
was like Gant was making us help him punish them boys cause
we keep quiet. After the whupping was over, I couldn't look at
the man or even the kids. I got up out of that little desk and went
out to the car. I set there in the car for over an hour before the
others come out.

Somehow or other, it dawned on me that I jist didn't see the
value in what we was doing—especially what I was doing. A
shikepoke like Smight can git paid to learn Indian languages and
things, and Indian kids git whupped for talking it. I hate to say it,
but I was out-and-out rude while we was driving back to D.C.
Whenever Smight or Overstreet happen to ast me any questions
about anything, I jist flat-out ignored them. Bledsoe, he seem to
know I was bothered, so he never intruded on my silence. I set
there in that front seat jist looking out at all the rich farms and
farm lands, all the big brick buildings and little white houses in

the little towns we passed through, and I never said a single solitary word while Smight and Overstreet talked about what grants they was trying to scare up in The Name of Science.

That night, after I had packed my bags, I walked the twenty blocks over to Dr. Payne's house. His maid, Selma, let me in and she tell me he was in a real bad way, that he taken a turn for the worse. But she say he want to talk to me. I go into his room, and he was laying on a daybed in pajamas. Books and papers are scattered all around and I can see that he is awful weak and that he has aged a lot since I last seen him.

"Thomas," he say. "Come sit down over here by me. I'm not hearing too good these days."

I do that, and I say that I hope he is feeling better.

"No, Thomas, I'm not," he say. "But for someone who's eighty-one, and who's had relatively good health almost all of his life, I'm not complaining." He try to set up a little bit, and I help him git comfortable. "But tell me, Thomas, how are you? Dr. Bledsoe was by earlier, and he told me that he thought you might be planning to leave. Is that true?"

"Yes sir, Dr. Payne. I be going back home now."

Then I went on to talk about missing the winter hunting and trapping and all. He listened politely, then he say, "Sometimes scientists and scholars kill the very things they love, don't they, Thomas?"

I stop, then look right at him and forgit about talking to him about hunting and what-all.

"Yes, sir. That is really right."

"Thomas, I could go on at length about the old adage of the

often necessary action of breaking eggs in order to make omelets, but I don't expect any of it will matter any. Am I right?"

"Yes, sir. I jist think I be tired of seeing too many people be the eggs you talk about."

"I agree with you, Thomas." He stopped and taken a drank of water from a glass by his bed. "Sometimes I have been very much discouraged by the Mr. Gants in the world and—I apologize for speaking disparagingly about colleagues—the Dr. Smights. But then we must remember the Dr. Bledsoes. And, most of all, Thomas, I remember that there are people like you." He look straight at me and took my hand in his. "You are a good man, Thomas. Your grandpapa and parents would be proud of you. You are a great Ofo."

I return the compliment to him, but he sort of wave it away.

"You know, Thomas, you are right. Your work is done here. You know that as well as I do."

"Thank you, sir. You been a great friend to me and I never will forgit that."

"Maybe your work was done even before you came here."

I couldn't answer that, so I jist set quiet and kind of nodded my head.

"Before you go, Thomas, I'd like you to have this," and he taken the old switch-cane Ofo flute out of a paper sack setting by his pillow. I start to say something about why I oughten not to taken something that belonged to the museum, but he shushed me and say, "No, Thomas. It's yours. I had Dr. Bledsoe go back and get it. We both want you to have it."

We joke a little about Dr. Smight having a litter of kittens when he find the flute is gone, and Dr. Payne say, "Let him. Let him even come down to Louisiana and hunt you up to get it back. I can see him now, out there trying to pole a skiff on your bayou, or wading through the swamps, looking for you. No, he won't bother you."

I smile at what he is saying.

"Remember, Thomas," he say as I am leaving. "You are an entire nation. No nation anywhere could have a better representative."

"I feel the same toward you, sir. Good-bye, sir."

"Good-bye, Thomas."

Before I was due to catch the bus to Louisiana at midnight, I stopped off at Melba's house. I ast if she was interested in pulling up stakes and coming along with me, either right then or later on. She say no, say too many of her family—kids and grandkids and all—was there around her in D.C. I figgered she was going to say that, so I told her that if anytime she want to come down to visit, or even to stay, she is always welcome. She say she jist might do that, but I think we both knowed then that she never would.

"Good-bye, Tom. You've been an awfully good friend," she say, and I think she emphasize "friend" in a real special way. Then she say, "Tom, you the lonesomest man I've ever known."

"Good-bye, Melba. Take good care of yourself."

Jist after I git back home, I spent some time telling my life story to a new tape recorder I got before I leave Washington. While I was still in Washington, I got a phone call from the Tunica Chief, and when I told him I was headed home, he ast me to make some tapes. Chief Joe say that they'd be for all our cousins and relations so they could hear the famous local guy—what Chief Joe call me—who went to Washington, D.C., to hobnob with the bigwigs. One night, when I had done used up a lot of tape, I walked outside my house in the pitch-dark and down the bayou bank to the water. I waded out into the bayou till I was in halfway up to my knees. In the dark, I had to be careful not to stumble over cypress knees or sunk dead tree limbs. Winter was jist about over, and it was still too early for moccasins and frogs and such to be out, but I could hear some herons and other kind of nightbirds making they sounds. And I heared a plover call. Some kind of little animal—a coon or a possum or a fieldrat—rustled a trail through the dry rushes and sedge at the bayou's edge and plunked into the water. I couldn't tell what it was, but I could see its ripples when it swum. The big white round moon was shining about two hand-breaths above the tree line and also in the bayou water in front of me. It was like a nighttime reminder of Sun Father's promise. For a little while I try to play the switch-cane flute, but I know I got a lot of practicing to do before I git the hang of it. Then I begin to talk real low and slow in Mosopelea. I had a great-big lump in my throat, and soon my low-talking become kind of loud, and then I wudn't so much singing as yelling. My face and eyes was wet, but I keep on singing till my voice become raspy, like a old lady's with a real-bad cold. I was beginning to git tired and also kind of chilly, but I sung on, and the lump got smaller and smaller and then it was gone. When I finally stopped, it seem to me like I could still hear me in all the trees around and out over the water. I turned and walked back to the bank, and I knowed pretty good that things was alright for the time being. But, if they wudn't, then I figgered I could come back out here tomorrow night and sing again.

At Ofo Town and Back into the Earth

An obituary from *Contemporary Anthropology*:

Last Ofo Speaker Dies

Thomas Darko, 92, of Sherrillton, La., informant of the late
Dr. William Allerton Payne and the late Dr. Matthew B.
Smight of the Smithsonian Institution, passed away on
Tuesday, October 14, 1997, of an undisclosed illness. Mr.
Darko, generally acknowledged to be the last surviving
member of the Ofo Tribe, was also the last remaining
speaker of the tribe's language. Several dozen members of
the Tunica-Biloxi Tribe, located predominantly near Sherrillton, are people with varying degrees of Ofo blood, but the
tribe itself now ceases to exist with Mr. Darko's passing.

Mr. Darko was born March 23, 1905, in the Tunica-
Biloxi tribal community located two miles outside Sherrillton, the son of the late Baptiste and Josephine Darko. His
grandfather, Louis Arceneaux, was regarded as the last
chief of the Ofo Tribe, an office he held until his death in
1922. Chief Arceneaux was an official in the Tunica-Biloxi
Tribe as well. Mr. Darko served in the U.S. Marines in

World War II and saw action in the Pacific Theater. From 1963 to 1964 he was employed by the Smithsonian Institution as a consultant on his tribal language, a position he abruptly terminated in 1964 for reasons unknown and, according to Dr. Smight, with much highly important work on an Ofo dictionary left uncompleted. A story circulates that, from the time he returned to Louisiana after his stay in Washington up until his death, Mr. Darko was never known to have uttered a single Ofo word publicly.

Mr. Darko leaves no surviving relatives except for distant cousins in the Tunica-Biloxi Tribe. Interment took place on October 16 at the old Ofo cemetery at Sherrillton.

About the Author

G eary Hobson (Cherokee-Quapaw/Chickasaw) is a professor of English, specializing in Native American literature, at the University of Oklahoma. His work appears in *Returning the Gift: Poetry and Prose from the First North American Native Writers' Festival,* edited by Joseph Bruchac (University of Arizona Press, 1994). He is the author of *Deer Hunting and Other Poems* (1990) and the editor of *The Remembered Earth: An Anthology of Contemporary Native American Literature* (1979). Since 1991 he has served as the project historian for "Returning the Gift," otherwise known as the "Native Writers Circle of the Americas."